After

© 2008 Smith, Bonappétit & Son,
Montréal (Canada), Hazel Hutchins

Legal Deposit: 3rd quarter 2008
Bibliothèque et Archives nationales
du Québec
Library and Archives Canada

The publisher wishes to acknowledge
the support of The Canada Council for
the Arts for this publishing program.
We are also thankful to the SODEC.

Government of Quebec—Tax credit
for book publishing—Administered
by SODEC

This publication was supported by a
grant from the Ontario Arts Council.

ISBN: 978-1-897118-42-9

After
Editor: Valérie Viel
Design: Andrée Lauzon
Copy Editor: Carolyn Jackson
Proofreader: Angèle Trudeau

Distributor for Canada:
University of Toronto Press

Printed in Canada by Transcontinental
Métrolitho.

**Bibliothèque et Archives nationales
du Québec and Library and Archives
Canada cataloguing in publication**

Hutchins, H. J. (Hazel J.)

After: a novel
(Spoonful fiction)

ISBN: 978-1-897118-42-9

I. Title.

PS8565.U826A62 2008
C813'.54   C2008-941681-3
PS9565.U826A62 2008

Hazel Hutchins

After
A novel

Smith, Bonappétit & Son

"… how we survive, when more than we had dreamt of is given, for no reason, and for no reason taken away."

— from "Evensong" by Peter Kane Dufault

1

Dear Amy,

You said once that being best friends meant we could tell each other things, anything, always. That's why I'm writing. More than anything in the world, there are things I need to tell my best friend.

Do you know where I am? I'm at Peter Limster's farm, the farm where he brings his dude ranch horses down from the mountains to spend the winter and now he's got show horses too, that stay year round. You came here with me one time. We climbed the big hill right to the top, where the grass smelled like sunshine and we could see forever. We talked about all the things we were going to do one day. One day. That was before I realized that one days don't happen.

Mom and Dad and I have moved here. Mom says that without Josh, Dad needs to get back to the country. Josh died at the Quick Mart. I guess you know that. Mom isn't telling anyone here. She says she feels better if nobody knows, as if it was his fault or something. It wasn't.

But this is the right place for keeping secrets. It's like being lost in time. There's no town, no supermarket, restaurant, or movie theatre. No mall, not even a small one.

There's just a store. It's called Four Corners and it's a fifteen-minute drive north of here. It's a tiny building with a single gas pump out front and a sign that reads "Credit Department 10th Floor." It took me three visits to understand what the sign meant, so you see I haven't gotten any smarter. Not that way, at least.

Further down the road is a school and across the road are a church and a community hall. That's all.

They have dances at the community hall, old time barn dances with fiddle music. I know because the neighbours invited us to one. Dad parked the car out front and we could hear the music, but neither Mom nor Dad opened their doors. They just sat there. And then Dad drove home.

No one feels like dancing.

Mom says Josh would have loved it here. She says he always loved it when we lived in the country. I don't remember. I was too little when we lived on our own farm, and there's a lot about Josh I didn't know.

How can that happen? How can there be things I didn't know about my own brother, things I'll never know?

I don't say that to Mom and Dad. When Mom says Josh would have loved it here I say "Yes, he would have," because it's probably true. And because Dad doesn't say anything at all.

Dad is training horses for Mr. Limster. They're Arabians, the kind you see in the movies racing across the desert with their necks arched and their tails flying, except these are for the show ring. Dad works them in the riding ring on the flat below the house. Walk, trot, canter—the horses learning to respond so that it seems to happen almost by magic. I never knew until we moved here how good Dad was with horses.

I ride too. There's nothing else to do. There's a horse named Nelson that I ride bareback in the little pasture beside the barn. He was bought a few weeks ago because he's gentle and can be used next year at the dude ranch but it didn't make sense to truck him to the mountains this late in the season. Mom makes a big deal about how I'm learning to ride, but to tell you the truth, it's boring. Nelson wanders around eating and I sit on top of him. Big deal. Mom would know that if she wanted to.

One minute, Amy, I want to be the best kid Mom and Dad could ever have. Because I have to be. Because there's only me. But the next minute I'm doing crazy stuff, getting mad and shouting and slamming doors. Back in the city I started hanging out with Lacy and her group, kids I don't really like, just because I didn't want to be alone.

I can't even do that any more. Not out here. Out here I really am alone. Even the Internet is back in the dark ages—dinosaur dial up, or at least that's Mom's excuse for not getting us connected.

Mom says we're doing all right. That's what she tells Aunt Stella when Stella phones about two million times a week. Mom tells her about the pottery studio she's setting up in the basement. She tells Stella how well Dad's doing with the horses. She tells Stella I'm excited about starting school next week.

I'm not excited, I'm scared. It was bad enough going back to school the first time, after. Kids I knew acted like I had some sort of disease. Kids I didn't know came up and wanted to know things, things you don't want to hear about. And adults kept telling me they knew how I felt.

No one knows how I feel.

Sometimes, when it gets really bad, I pretend it didn't happen. I sit in my room and close my eyes and pretend the world hasn't changed. I pretend that everything is like before. Or even better, I pretend I'm in our old house and Josh is downstairs eating breakfast. I get out of bed and go down and say to him, "Josh, I've just had a dream and something bad's going to happen if you go to work today. So don't."

He doesn't. He phones the people who own the store and tells them about my dream. His warning helps them stop the worst parts from happening. The next day we see pictures in the newspaper of all the shattered glass, but we read that no one was hurt and we're so glad. So glad.

Since we've moved, I can't even trick myself into pretending any more.

Tomorrow I start school. If I can just write to you about things—about my new school, about things that happen—maybe it will help. Just to have someone on my side, the way it used to be.

I wish you were here.

I wish you were here.

I wish you were here.

Kate

2

When he wakes, he already knows he's running late, knows from the sounds of the city seeping through the fourth-floor window of the apartment—the *beep beep beep* of the garbage truck at the dumpster, the way the early rush of traffic has settled to a hum.

He climbs into the clothes he laid out last night, a black T-shirt and jeans, the kind that can carry you through the week when you need them to. The sounds of breathing are loud beyond the wall that separates the bedrooms.

"Mom!" he calls. "Wake up Cleo."

By the time he comes out of the bathroom, his little sister is standing outside, hopping from one foot to the other.

"We have to hurry," he tells her.

She nods and scurries past him.

He opens the fridge, more out of habit than hope. The milk carton is empty, he knows that without picking it up, but beside it are two sandwiches wrapped tightly in plastic, cafeteria style. He's glad to see them. The teachers will watch out for Cleo at the little kids' school, slip her something extra from the food they keep in the staffroom if she needs it, but he's pretty sure no one slips a kid any food at A. R. Winston Junior High. At Winston he'll be on his own in more ways than one.

He puts one sandwich in Cleo's backpack and one in his own. They leave together. He gets Cleo across the busy street and watches until she turns the corner that's just a block from the school the way he told his mom he would.

He looks up the street, sees the number 18 bus coming, and catches it at the stop on the corner just before it turns up the hill. Most of the kids from his old school chose the junior high further downtown, but Winston's not much further and you get the bus tickets free either way.

When he gets to the school, kids are streaming in from all directions. He's not as late as he thought he'd be and he knows the layout of the building from spring orientation. Still, by the time he finds his homeroom, the only seats left are at the very front. He hesitates in the doorway, thinks maybe this wasn't such a good idea after all, but the teacher's already spotted him and is waving him in. Two kids from the hallway push through. He makes himself saunter in behind them, slides into one of the front seats, and slouches down so he's not so tall.

"If you lose your lock, it's thirty dollars," the teacher is saying, slapping sheets down on their desks to fill out and sign. "If you lose the combination, it's five dollars because they're stored in the office and no one wants to be looking them up every thirty seconds."

"I hate the front row," whispers a voice beside him.

A girl with long, brown hair is grimacing as she slides into the seat next to his.

He nods, thinks about saying something, but hesitates. He feels something along the back of his neck. Eyes watching him. He shifts in his seat, knocks the paper to the floor, does a quick look back as he picks it up.

In the back row is a kid who's looking at him, hard. He sinks a little lower. It's probably nothing. Probably someone who remembers him from a thousand years ago when he played hockey. Or maybe someone who thinks he's another kid entirely. Let it roll right by you, he tells himself. When you start to think everyone's watching you, it's the beginning of the end.

They have three classes in homeroom. For Math and Science they switch to rooms down the hall, the same kids but at least he's able to snag a seat in the back. They won't start options until next week.

Lunch isn't exactly fun, but on the first day of school he's not the only one trying to be invisible. There's only one bad moment, that's when he sees Chalmers leaning against a locker down one of the halls at the other end of the school. What's he doing here? Of all the kids at his old school, he'd have expected Chalmers to have gone downtown. He doesn't ask. Finds another hallway. There are lots of hallways where you can lose yourself. He's careful on the way home to make sure they're not both on the same bus.

"I've got Miss Winters," Cleo calls out as soon as he walks in the door. "She's new. She's really pretty and she says I'm good at printing."

"New" is good, he thinks. "New" can't already have labels made up for Cleo for things she hasn't done.

"Did you find your classes?" asks his mom. "Are you with anyone you know?"

He shrugs.

"I made out OK," he says. "Couple of my teachers might not be too bad."

She's not quite listening somehow. She's told him so many times over the years "you're not the one I have to worry about, Sam" that she's come to believe it. Besides, she's got the bus to catch to work and is already putting on her coat.

"There's food in the fridge," she says. "Spaghetti for supper. I'll try to phone at my break."

They turn on the TV as soon as she's out the door.

3

Dear Amy,

Today I was swallowed by a whale.

OK, not exactly, but that's what it feels like to climb into a big, empty school bus that goes on forever.

The bus driver is the same neighbour who asked us to the dance. Her name is Mrs. Gilbert and I could tell by the way she swung the door lever shut that she'd done it a million times before. Her little boy sat in the seat behind her. He has a round face like the moon, enormous blue eyes, and freckles scattered all across his cheeks like cookie crumbs. I didn't know what to do, so I sat across from him.

Behind me was the rest of the bus, empty seats marching down to the back like ribs inside a whale. For a long time that's all of us there seemed to be in the whole universe, we three humans inside a whale swimming past hills and fields and little treed valleys so early the sun hadn't touched them yet.

"Hello there, Twyla. Have you met Kate from down the road?"

That's what Mrs. Gilbert said at the next stop when a girl about my age climbed onto the bus. She had spiked hair and thirteen layers of black eyeliner. I didn't expect to meet someone with spiked hair out here. Twyla said hi, but she didn't sit with me. I guess she thought I looked too normal or something. She swung on down the ribs and landed in a seat at the very back.

After that the bus went up and down all sorts of little

side roads and hills, picking up kids at farms I hadn't even known were there. They were mostly little kids. The seats filled up two by two and there I was still sitting alone.

At last two brothers got on. Same hair cuts. Same eyes. Same jackets, lunch boxes, and running shoes. They sat down beside me. I could look right over their heads, that's how little they were.

You would have liked them. You would have nicknamed them Bob 1 and Bob 2 and you would have told them jokes and had them playing rock, paper, scissors in no time. No one would have even known that you were the new kid.

I wanted to be that way, but I can't, Amy. I can't without you. So I sat there and felt more and more miserable, even though I tried not to show it, especially when some older boys got on toward the end of the route.

It took more than an hour to get to school because of all the side roads we had to take. I thought we'd never get there, then suddenly the bus was pulling into the school-yard and everyone was piling out and meeting up with other kids from other buses and going into the school. I don't remember exactly how I found the right classroom except there's only one class for each grade so I guess it wasn't that hard.

A girl named Carolyn found me a desk. Actually, she found me first and then she found us a locker and then she found the desk. She's got thick, curly hair that she wants to cut and glasses that she's going to get rid of some day, and I'm not sure whether she's super kind or just likes to organize people. I don't care either.

A couple of other girls talked to me. There's one named

Ellie who moves so quietly and talks so softly she's practically invisible. She said she lives near me, but she's on a different bus route. She asked if I had a horse. I didn't know what to say. I'm not entirely sure Nelson is a real horse, and he's not exactly mine.

There's a girl named Jade who has long, blond hair. All the boys like her—it takes about three minutes to figure that one out. She asked if she could borrow my pencil crayons. And my eraser. And my water bottle. And a bunch of other stuff. Jade the Borrower. I learned at recess that she's good friends with Twyla from the bus. Twyla's one year older. From my desk I could see her spikes in the room across the hall.

As I sat there looking at Twyla's spikes and waiting for the teacher, I began to wonder what it would be like if this was just the first day of class, I mean if it was before and we'd just moved here. How would I have felt? Would I have been as scared? Would the kids have treated me differently? What would it really have felt like?

My heart began beating about a zillion times a minute when the teacher arrived. Maybe I knew what was going to happen next. Maybe I didn't. She's the kind of teacher who wears high heels and lipstick and smiles a lot. I didn't know they still had those kinds of teachers in junior high. When she called the roll you could tell she knew everyone, everyone except me.

"You're new, Kate," she said. "Tell us something about yourself."

So there I was with everyone looking at me like I was some kind of exhibit. What was I supposed to say?

"Your report card is from the city. Is that where you grew up?" asked the teacher.

"Yes," I said.

"Is your family going to farm now?" she asked.

"My dad's training horses," I said.

"Do you have any brothers and sisters?" she asked.

Even though, way deep down, I'd known it would happen sooner or later, it took me by surprise. It took me by surprise like a freight train that you see coming a long way off but you don't realize until the last minute that you're standing right on the tracks.

She didn't even know what she was asking. She just stood up there smiling, not knowing. It's a question I've been asked lots of times, Amy. Lots of times. But it was always before. Now it's a thousand miles from before, and I didn't know what to say. It was awful. The longer I waited the more awful it got. I had to say something but I couldn't say no. I couldn't, Amy.

"Just me," I said.

Just me. I felt like I'd screamed the words, but I guess I hadn't because everyone was still sitting there looking at me like everything was normal. Normal. And the teacher kept asking questions.

"Do you have any pets? Any hobbies? Do you like any special subjects in school?"

I said I have three elephants that bungee jump and a walrus that helps me solve math puzzles. At least that's what I wish I'd said. It's nobody's business.

There was another part that didn't go very well. I have a confession to make. I wore a dress. It was a dumb, little-kid thing to do, first day of school in my new dress. I don't know why I did it.

And do you remember in grade five—not even last year but in grade five!—how we always had to stand by our desk when we spoke. We all had to do it, so it didn't seem weird or anything, but here no one does it except for you-know-who, your best friend, Kate, who suddenly was back in grade five, popping to attention by her desk.

I tried not to. I really did. I could see that none of the other kids were doing it and every time I stood up I felt taller and taller in my stupid dress until I seemed to be towering miles above everyone.

At last some boy called from the back of the room.

"Hey, you don't have to stand up every time you answer a question, you know!"

I turned around to look at him. He was in a desk way at the back corner of the room, kind of a rumpled looking kid with blond hair and a sideways grin. If I'd had magic powers he would have been gone in an instant. Zap.

But the funny thing is after he spoke, after he said what everyone else including the teacher was thinking but was too embarrassed or too polite to say out loud, it was better. I was able to answer questions sitting down. Pretty soon after that, instead of feeling like I was in grade five, I felt like I was way past all of them, in high school or something, older than anyone else in the room. So long as I was just watching, so long as I didn't have to say anything or answer questions but could just watch, I felt they were a whole lot younger than me and didn't know anything at all.

So I survived, at least as far as getting through the rest of the day without answering more questions. Half the time I let Carolyn organize me and the other half of the time I pretended I wasn't there at all. In the bus on the way home I sat in the same seat with Bob 1 and Bob 2. Once you've chosen your seat, that's where you sit for the rest of the year. And then I got off the school bus and walked up the lane.

The lane is beautiful. At the bottom are two great cottonwood trees that look like giants on sentry duty. They seemed to be waiting for me. As I passed between them and began to climb the hill, the carrigana bushes closed in on either side, almost touching overhead. It was secretive and safe; and I thought, just for a minute, it's all right. It's going to be alright.

But when I reached the very top and was almost in the yard, I knew. It was like crossing an invisible line from the outside world, and I knew.

It's not going to be all right. Nothing fits together any more. Dad and the horses. Mom and the studio. And way off in left field somewhere, me and Nelson. And now there's school, too.

It's like a photograph. It doesn't matter if it's a photograph of the city or a photograph of the farm, there's a big hole in it. A big hole in it where Josh used to be.

I'm so angry, Amy. I'm so mad I want to scream and cry and yell. I'm mad at the guy himself, the guy whose name I don't ever want to know. I'm so mad at him there isn't a word for it.

And I'm mad at everyone else too. I'm mad at the people who own the shop and the people on the street and the police and the ambulance driver and Mom and Dad and every nurse and doctor in the hospital, because they didn't stop it from happening or fix it when it did. It's not even their fault and I'm mad at them! I wasn't angry at them before!

I'm going to tell Mom. I'm going to tell her we have to go back to the city. She says this is a new start for all of us, but it isn't working. It's making things worse.

I'm going to tell Mom.

I hope I can think up the right words.

4

"You time it exactly don't you?" says the girl at the next desk. "You arrive one nanosecond before the bell."

She's right. By the end of the week, he's got the timing figured out. He did himself a favour that first day, catching the late bus. It's the one he takes every morning now. If he doesn't stop at his locker, he gets to class on time without running into Chalmers.

Once he's in class he can almost relax. The kid at the back of the room still watches him, but he hasn't said anything so it must be the way he thought it was the first day. It must be about something else, something that doesn't have anything to do with Everett and the Quick Mart. But he's still careful to learn the kid's name—John—from the teacher doing roll call.

He learns the name of the girl at the next desk from roll call, too. It's Helen and she likes to talk. She tells him she moved here from a little town up north. When she discovers that one of her option choices has been cancelled because everyone has to take French, no exceptions, she's totally disgusted.

"I don't need French class! Where I come from everyone speaks French!"

She says her great-grandmother can barely say three words of English but that most people are like she is, French or English, whatever they need to speak.

He doesn't believe her. He's never heard of places like that in the West and can't hear even the trace of an accent.

Then he overhears her between classes talking to *Maman* on her cell phone. The words flow a mile a minute. Yup. She can speak French.

"You'll get a great mark. You won't even have to work at it," he tells her.

"I'll go insane if I have to listen to all of you mispronounce words only a two-year-old would use," she says. "It's bad enough that no one around here even tries to say my name right."

Her name is Helen. How can you not say it right? He doesn't ask.

His options have been switched around too, not because of French but because too many kids signed up for photography. He's been slotted into Woodworking instead. It's at the other end of the school where the Industrial Arts classes are held, where he saw Chalmers hanging out. Not good, but there's nothing he can do about it and options don't start until the middle of next week. Way too far ahead to worry.

For now, at least, he's got a way of avoiding Chalmers after school. He leaves by the back door, walks six blocks in the opposite direction and waits for the next bus on the schedule. It's only a ten-minute wait and he can ride home without any other kids around at all.

But today is Friday and classes end early. He turns directly for home along the side streets. Maybe he can walk all the way and save a bus ticket.

5

Dear Amy,

For three days Mom's been lying on the sofa, with the curtains pulled and the lights off. She gets up to make supper and then lies down again while Dad and I eat. It's like she's holding up a big sign, I feel worse than you. How can there be worse? How can there be worse when the hurting is so bad you can't stand it.

I didn't talk to her.

This morning was better. It's Saturday and the sound of the vacuum woke me up and then it was right in my room.

"Aunt Stella just phoned. She'll be here in an hour, Kate," Mom called over the sound of the vacuum eating my socks. "How about picking things up."

I don't know how Mom can be like that, one minute collapsed on the sofa and the next minute moving at the speed of light, as if nothing's wrong. I wasn't going to get up. I was going to stay in bed forever and let the socks take over the world, until I thought about Dad. Dad and Stella don't always get along. Dad should know she was coming.

There was something else too, Amy. I was still half asleep, so I could imagine it almost as if it were real. I pictured Dad leaning at the side of the barn door with his bony legs and arms sticking out the way they do. I pictured me sitting on a bale of hay with my legs swinging, even though I'm way too tall for my legs to swing now, but kind of like before, way before, when I'd sit on the back steps when he was working on the truck.

"What's up Kat-kin?" he'd say, the way he used to. "Well Kat-kin, what's on your mind?"

"We need to go back to the city," I'd say. "We never should have moved. You don't move when something horrible happens. It's horrible enough without moving."

"Alright," he'd say. "Alright. We'll go back."

That's what I pictured happening.

When I got there, there weren't any bales to sit on, and Dad wasn't leaning against the barn door. He was feeding the horses and he barely stopped long enough for me to tell him Stella was coming. He didn't ask what was on my mind. I didn't tell him.

I didn't know what to do after that. I didn't want to go back inside with Mom and the vacuum cleaner and all the other things she'd be doing as if they mattered. I started following Dad around.

Dad was in and out of the stalls, around and under and behind the horses. I've been in the barn before, of course, but I hadn't really watched what went on. Dad moves around horses as if they're old friends. He doesn't even seem to think about it. The horses don't think about it either, they just kind of ignore him. With me it's different. I always seem to be bumping into the horses or the stalls or myself. I guess I was bumping into Dad too, because he finally stopped and frowned at me. He took a bucket from its wall clip in the nearest stall.

"Rinse it out at the tap. Fill it up. Put it back," he said.

So I did. I couldn't heave a full bucket up to clip it on the wall again, but I figured out how to do half a bucket and then top it up. And then I filled up the buckets for the other five horses too, which was pretty brave because to tell you the truth, the Arabs are skittish and I'm scared of them, but they were busy eating so that helped.

After that I helped Dad brush the white mare. Her name's Sand Dancer. She's as beautiful as the others, but she's older and gentler. She's pregnant too, so maybe that's why she's quieter. I don't know. I don't know a whole lot about horses except their noses are incredibly soft and it hurts when they step on your toe, even by accident, and using a pitchfork to clean out a stall is harder than it looks because unless you manage to get a good lump of straw and horse manure all kind of wadded together it just falls through the tines of the fork. I learned that this morning.

Even with my help, the chores never did get done. Dad kept finding more to do.

"Go back to the house, Kate," he said at last. "Your aunt will want to see you."

Maybe it was true. Maybe it wasn't.

You've never met Aunt Stella. She's a lawyer and wears suit jackets with shoulder pads, even when she's wearing blue jeans. She has thick, shiny hair that falls like a curtain to cover her face when she leans forward. She leans forward a lot. Sometimes I really, really like her, but when she's in one of her pushy moods I don't want to be anywhere near her. Today was one of those days.

I don't understand, Amy. I'm the one who doesn't want to be here, but the moment I stepped into the house and heard Stella telling Mom we shouldn't have moved, it made me really mad. She was telling Mom all the things she was doing wrong, all the things she should be doing right, all the things she should be feeling. Why do people do that? Why do they think they know all about other people's lives? I'm never going to be like that. Never. I wanted to scream at her to let Mom alone. "You don't know!" I wanted to say. "You think you do, but you don't know!"

I went down to my room and slammed the door so hard the house rattled. I thought Mom would come after me for it but she didn't. Neither of them came after me and it made me wish I hadn't slammed it after all. That's the way it is with me, Amy—the good Kate and the bad Kate. Half the time I don't even know which is which.

After a while I heard them go downstairs. I knew Mom was showing Aunt Stella the pottery studio. It doesn't feel like a real studio yet. It's too clean. The studios Mom used to take me to when I was little would always be splattered with clay and glaze, and the tables would be worn with use. I'd build bowls out of coils or make pinch pots or just stand and watch her work the wheel round and round until the lump of wet clay became something entirely different, not more beautiful exactly, because clay itself is beautiful, but beautiful in a different way.

Those were some of the good times. Before. There were lots of good times before.

Now Mom has built her very own studio. She's done most of it herself, the benches and tables and shelves. An electrician helped her put in the kiln and the potter's wheel and extra lighting because there are only two small windows in the basement so she needs the lights on even in the daytime. She hasn't actually started making things there yet, that's why it doesn't quite feel like a studio. I guess Stella must have noticed it too.

"Do you think your mom will ever really work downstairs?" she asked when she finally cornered me after lunch.

"Sure," I said. "Why not?"

As soon as the words were out of my mouth I wanted to tell her I was sorry. I wanted to tell her I understood what she meant, that the way Mom's acting all brave and saying she's ready to make a new start is crazy, because that's not how she really feels at all. Inside she's broken up in a million pieces.

But it's all part of the game. We all have to keep pretending we're OK. How could I tell Stella something like that?

So I left it sounding like I don't care. Don't care about Mom. Or Dad. Don't even care about Josh.

Oh Amy, I do care. It's my fault I didn't know him better. It's my fault that when Mom does talk about him, when she just can't help it, when she says Josh would have liked this or liked that, I can't think of what to say.

And when she was lying on the couch all week I still couldn't think of what to say, even when I knew what was wrong, even when I knew she was thinking of Josh going off to school. Maybe she is thinking how it would have been this year, his final year, with graduation and all that goes with it. Maybe she was thinking how it used to be when he was little.

She told someone once what it was like the first day she sent him to school in his new blue jacket and his new red cap and the back of his neck so small as he walked away into the world. Why do I remember her telling someone that? I don't want to remember! I have enough of my own things to try to forget!

I'm sorry, Amy. I wasn't going to tell you all this. I was just going to tell you about the horses, about helping in the barn. That's the part you would have liked.

School again on Monday. I know it's wrong to look forward to something, but that's almost the way I feel, because at least I won't be here with Mom and Dad.

I'll tell you what happens.

Please don't be angry with me.

6

Things at school fall into a routine. English is going to be as boring as ever. The Social Studies teacher has a smoking habit that can't be masked by peppermints. Most of the kids are pretty clued in; a couple of sarcastic specialists, but the teachers seem to know when to shut it down. The Math teacher actually likes the subject. He brings in puzzles, challenges them to think of ways to measure the height of the tree outside the window without cutting it down.

They start a group project in Science and he gets along well with the couple of guys he's working with. They talk about signing up for house leagues when they start next week. He's good at sports. He's more hopeful than he's been in a long time.

And as soon as he thinks it, he feels guilty. Things aren't supposed to work out.

He needn't have worried. When he walks into the woodworking shop on Wednesday there stands Chalmers with a big grin on his face.

"Hey, Sammy, my friend! I thought you'd be taking nuclear science instead of cutting up wood with the rest of us."

Chalmers has a couple of sidekicks hovering close by. It looks like he's already building up his own little gang.

"He's a real brain is he?" asks one of the kids.

"Genuine Einstein?" asks the other.

"Oh he's smart, but that doesn't mean you want to mess with him. This is a kid with very interesting family connections," says Chalmers. "Right, Sammy?"

Chalmers' eyes are dark and bright with meaning. Things don't really change, thinks Sam, don't ever get better. He might as well have gone to the school downtown, where everyone already knows.

Except he wouldn't have, even if he'd known that he'd run into Chalmers here. Everett went to school downtown.

He waits for Chalmers to tell his followers about Everett and the Quick Mart. He waits to see which expressions will show most strongly on the kids' faces—shock, disbelief, horror, disgust, or one he hates the most—a fearful awe.

But Chalmers' eyes are becoming hooded. An idea is forming in the strange channels of his brain, Sam realizes. Chalmers is weighing the idea, shifting it like a stone in the palm of his hand. Throw it now? Save it for later?

"Yeah?" presses one of the boys around him.

Chalmers has made his decision. He'll hold for now. "Oh yeah," he says, nodding wisely. "Very interesting family connections."

Sam doesn't like the feeling in the pit of his stomach. Chalmers is looking to play him for something. That's the only reason for him to hold back.

What could Chalmers want? He's never got any cash. He's never got anything else, for that matter. Chalmers must realize that. They've always gone to the same school. For a couple of years Chalmers even lived down the hall from Sam's apartment.

The others are waiting for an explanation, but Chalmers doesn't give in.

"You don't need to know," he tells the others, casually picking up a piece of wood. "Just take my word for it.

Everyone doesn't need to know everything. At least not right at this moment. Right, Sammy?"

WHAM

He makes the piece of wood slap down so hard and fast on the flat of the table that everyone jumps, even the kids who watched him do it. Two guys sitting with their backs to him practically fall off their chairs. Chalmers laughs, taking the attention away from where it was just a few seconds ago.

Sam's smart enough to know he shouldn't be grateful, but he is.

7

Dear Amy,

Yesterday I moved to the back of the bus. Twyla's the one who talked me into it.

"You may as well sit with me," is what she actually said, but it sounded better than that at the time. We're not supposed to move once we've chosen our seats for the year, but Mrs. Gilbert said she'd make an exception, since I didn't know anyone the first day.

It's better in the back. I'm not so sure about Twyla yet, but it's definitely better riding at the back. At the back you don't worry about whether or not anyone is looking at you. You watch the seats fill up in front of you on the way to school and on the way home you watch the seats empty one by one until only the ribs of the whale remain.

The bumps are biggest in the back of the bus. There's one near the end of the route that sends us flying in the air like little kids on a roller coaster. We're the big little kids in the back of the bus.

Twyla's "into" boys. In fact that's mostly what she talks about. Who she likes. Who she doesn't like. Who likes who. There are a couple of grade nine boys who get on and off close to the school, but the rest of the time there's just little kids around so she's pretty much free to talk all she wants. I just listen. You can learn a lot of things just listening and besides, the one time I asked about something she looked at me like I was crazy.

"Boy, are you dumb for a city kid," she said.

Which is true I guess, at least the way Twyla sees the world.

Making friends is something I'm trying to figure out. Do you remember how all those years I was best friends with Megan? She was tall and I was tall. She was smart in school and I was smart in school. Our mothers knew each other. We both couldn't run very fast. We both had straight, brown hair. It was like we had to be friends.

But we weren't. Not really. I didn't know that until you came along.

Do you want to know the truth? I was pretty surprised you wanted to be my friend. You were little and bouncy. I was big and boring. You talked the lady at the video store into letting us take out old releases for free, and the pool-room man into letting us play a game if it was quiet, and the girl who worked nights at the gas station into letting us hang out there and drink coffee, even though we weren't supposed to. I always told Mom I was going to the library. A lot of the time, when I was hanging out with you, I told Mom I was going to the library. She knew we were friends, but she didn't know how close we were. She didn't want to know. I can't tell her now.

Even your house was different from ours. It was always half dark inside with the drapes pulled and the TV on low. While I was waiting for you I'd make a game of watching the layers of cigarette smoke drift through the slices of sunlight that snuck between the curtains.

There was that guy with the ponytail, your mom's boyfriend, who hung around for a couple of months. The tattoo on his arm reminded me of the fancy lettering on the scroll in my doctor's office. And there were other guys too. I never asked you about them. I just let you tell me what you wanted to tell me. Lies or truth, it didn't matter. Maybe that's one of the reasons we were friends.

Twyla's mom and dad have been married forever, just like my mom and dad, so I don't see how she knows so much, but I guess she just does or maybe having an older sister helps. I don't mean about sex, I'm sure she knows more about sex than I do too, but it's pretty hard to talk about it in the back of the bus with little kids around. I just mean the "look around and figure out what's happening" everyday stuff.

"You know the girl in my class with the brown hair that's kind of frizzy? She thinks Gord likes her, but he doesn't."

That's what Twyla told me on the way home today. I think it means that Twyla likes Gord, but I'm not sure. One of the rules around here seems to be that you never really say who you like just in case they don't like you back. Actually, that seemed to be one of the rules in the city, too. I just never thought about it before.

The boy who told me I don't have to stand up all the time, the one with the rumpled clothes, is named Ryland. He's kind of a weird kid. He's smart when he wants to be smart, but the rest of the time he just kind of sits at the rear of the class and watches the world go by like he's watching TV or something. Sometimes you get the feeling that he'd like to change the channel.

I would have liked to change the channel today. I started crying in the middle of Math. I'm such a geek. There was a dumb question about how old someone's brother would be on his sister's twelfth birthday if he was double her age on her sixth birthday, and I just started crying.

I left the room before it got really bad. The teacher is a real Ms. Helpful and followed me into the hall. I told her I had a bad stomachache. "I'll call your mom to come get you," said Ms. Helpful.

"My mom's not home," I lied. "She's in the city today. So is my dad." As if my mom and dad ever do anything together any more.

Ms. Helpful made me go down to the school's sick room. It's about the size of a closet, way at the other end of the school in the little kid's wing. There's a weight scale and an eye chart and a bed, like a prison cot. Actually the whole room is a lot like a prison room or a hospital room for people going crazy.

Am I going crazy, Amy? How does a person know if they're going crazy or not? Just because you feel one way does it mean it's really happening? Is there something to do to stop it? Does it ever stop?

The teacher sent Jade to check on me at recess. I thought it would be Carolyn, but Jade came instead. I wondered what she would want to borrow this time. People in the loony bin don't have much to lend.

"Can I get you a glass of water?" she asked.

"I'm better," I said. "I'll be OK soon."

Jade looked relieved. I don't think playing sick nurse is really her thing.

But just before she left, she said something I wasn't expecting. She'd already turned away, so I wasn't sure whether she was talking to me or to the door at first.

"I felt like crying all last year, especially the first couple of months," she said. "I mean I know you weren't crying, you just had a stomachache, but in case you ever do feel like crying, you should know that moving does that to you, except of course I'm not allowed to cry."

It was better after recess. I went back to class and I didn't start crying again.

And it really is better riding at the back of the bus. Even Bob 1 and Bob 2 look happier now that I'm not sitting with them any more.

I didn't ask Jade what she meant about not being allowed to cry.

8

He hears kids talking at school about all the things they're doing after class, all the things they're planning to do on the weekend. His life isn't nearly that complicated.

School.

Home.

School.

Home.

Not a lot in between.

Sometimes he gets a vague sense that he should be feeling left out, should be growing restless. He doesn't feel that way. He's in some kind of limbo, a "between" spot that's muffled from the sounds and sensations beyond.

There have always been these quieter times, times when Everett withdrew into himself and they all briefly lived in almost the same way as everyone else. Times, even after he'd moved out, when their mother said, "Everett's getting his life together, Sam. I talked to him today. He sounded good."

And then the next moment it would all split apart with a call from the police or the emergency department saying to come and get him, or Everett himself banging on the door.

Of course he knows that's changed. He knows that if the phone rings or the door opens now, it won't be Everett.

But it's complicated. The between times have never lasted before. Why should he trust life now? It's easier to think of something else entirely.

Bonjour, Paul. Bonjour, Hélène.

He's watching TV with Cleo because when you're in limbo, it doesn't matter what you stare at on the screen. It's one of her little kids' shows. Puppets with green hair and purple skin talking French. He hears them with his English ears.

He knows they are saying hello but he doesn't recognize the names until—lime green with orange polka dots—the words flash on the screen.

Bonjour, Paul. Bonjour, Hélène.

He starts to pay attention. Maybe there's a different way to say Helen after all.

9

Dear Amy,

Mom has started working in the studio. I feel like phoning up Aunt Stella and saying, "I told you so" except now that she's started, it's like the studio has swallowed her. She's always down there. Sometimes she comes up for supper. Other times I come home from school and find a note asking me to warm up something for Dad and me that's already in the fridge. We're getting good at eating in front of the TV.

This morning, when the magpies woke me up early (it's Saturday and people should be allowed to sleep in, but I guess the magpies don't know that), I tried to go down to see what she was working on. The door was locked. Why would anyone put a lock on a door in the basement?

So I went out to the barn and helped Dad do the chores again. At least I kind of knew what to do this time. Sand Dancer and I are getting to be friends.

"You can brush Calypso while you're at it, Kate," Dad called as he pushed the wheelbarrow down the alley between the stalls.

I pretended I didn't hear him. Calypso is young and nervous and moves around the stall thumping her hooves and tossing her mane. But Dad stuck his head over the stall a few moments later.

"You can brush Calypso too, Kate," he said again.

I finished brushing Sand Dancer, gave her a pat for good luck and went across to Calypso's stall.

"Hello girl. I'm just here to scratch your back."

I read somewhere that you're supposed to talk to horses and you're supposed to move slowly and gently. Very gently I undid the stall latch. Very slowly I moved into her stall.

"OK, see. Here's the brush. Do you want to smell it? Now I'm just going to brush you very gently. Very, very gently here on the neck and…"

"What are you doing, Kate?" Dad's voice was so loud over my shoulder it made me jump. "You'll make that mare nervous fooling around like that. Brush her good and hard."

I brushed her good and hard. I made myself do it. She did a bit of a sideways dance with her rump, but she didn't flatten me against the wall or trample me so I guess we made out OK.

Just as I finished, Dad brought in the tack. I was afraid he was going to ask me to saddle her up—I have enough trouble getting the bridle over Nelson's head and he's asleep most of the time—but Dad stepped in and took over.

As I watched him, I began to think I'd seen it all before. *Déjà vu*, isn't that what they call it? Only it wasn't quite right. Something was off. I stood there looking at Dad. He held his head a certain way, tilted at a funny little angle the way he does when he's working with his hands, and every once in a while he seemed to hesitate, as if he was waiting for someone to hand him what he needed next, hand it to him without even asking.

And then I knew. Josh and Dad used to work on the truck together that way. It was as if for a moment I could see Josh there too, holding his head at the same angle, handing things to Dad. I felt queasy and sick and cold all over.

The next thing I knew, I was out in the sunshine sitting on the stack of bales behind the barn. I must have climbed up there myself. I don't remember.

Why wasn't it me, Amy? Why am I still here and Josh isn't? It would have been better the other way around. Josh would have known what to hand Dad. He would have known how to work a pitchfork. He wouldn't have been afraid of the horses. And when Mom feels so bad about all the firsts, the first day of school, the first visit to the mountains, the first bicycle, it's always Josh she's remembering. You always remember the first time the best. I'm just Kate who came second.

Dad doesn't talk about missing Josh. He doesn't hide in the bedroom on bad days, turn into wonder-woman when Aunt Stella arrives, or lock himself in the basement, but it's every bit as bad. Part of him has just been wiped away, a great huge part of him, but the crazy thing is it only shows up in the smallest ways. He doesn't joke around any more. And he doesn't whistle. And he calls me Kate.

That's all right. I don't feel like Kat-kin any more. I feel a lot older than that.

And I don't care that no one noticed the social studies project I left spread on the table after I worked on it all afternoon. I'm not going to finish it. It won't make any difference to the world whether I finish it or not.

Tomorrow I'm going to sleep late and watch TV all day.

I don't care.

I don't care.

I don't care.

10

"If you run into someone you know, ask them over!"

His mom gets weekends off, it's why she took the night job, one of the reasons anyway. Most of the time she's too tired to do much more than catch up on laundry, help Cleo with her reading, sort through bills, shop for groceries.

This Saturday, though, she's having one of her other weekends, a burst of energy that can't be contained, and she's making the most of it—cleaning the living room and kitchen from top to bottom, taking Cleo to the park just to run through the leaves and dragging him along too. Sunday she tackles the bedrooms, tells them to have friends over. Cleo knows two little girls just around the corner and within five minutes the living room is full of dolls and toy ponies and singing pigs. Sam clears out, says he's got places to go.

There's a library just past the park where you can sign up for computers, and they don't care if all you do is play games on them. It's supposed to be only for a half hour at a time, but if it's not busy they don't bother to kick you off.

He's halfway there when he hears a voice.

"Hey Sammy boy!"

Chalmers falls into step beside him. Sam nods, but doesn't say anything. Chalmers is good at talking.

"Don't see you around much, 'cept in class. You should come find us at school at noon. Out in the parking lot. There's a couple of good guys I hang out with."

Sam nods again in a noncommittal way.

"You still living in the same apartment?

"Yeah," says Sam.

"That wasn't such a bad place," says Chalmers "'cept the walls were thin. I sure knew that from living down the hall. Your brother really used to get going sometimes, didn't he? The whole place could hear him yelling."

"That was a long time ago." Sam shrugs, as if to show that the time Chalmers is talking about is so far off his radar it doesn't register. "Last couple of years, he wasn't around much."

Chalmers eyes him, seems to want to say one thing, decides to say something different instead.

"You know that house on the corner that's boarded up?" he asks. "How 'bout you and I do some exploring? Bet we could find some interesting stuff in there."

"Not today," says Sam.

"You afraid? Boogie-man scare you?" Chalmers fake-punches him in the arm. "Course you're not afraid. You're like your brother. Anyone bothers us, I'll clue them in about who they're messing with. You can trust me."

Sam doesn't bite.

"Not today," he says.

He thinks Chalmers will keep pushing, but maybe he was just ragging on him all along because all he does is smile.

"Suit yourself," he says. "I got some school supplies to pick up anyway. Want to help out? They're making store clerks dumber and dumber these days, but it's easier with two."

Sam knows the game but he's not playing. Chalmers turns off when they reach the corner. Sam keeps walking.

He's not headed for the library any more. Maybe it's

because of meeting up with Chalmers or maybe he wasn't headed there in the first place.

He walks and walks and walks. West on 45th Street. Across the river. Up into the streets beyond. It's all houses here. Trees and yards. Not new, but not old either. Mostly he sticks to the busier streets, but sometimes he has to cut across a few blocks through the houses.

When he reaches 182nd Avenue, he's not sure if he needs to go north or south. He stands looking, first one direction and then the other. He guesses north. Walks past the gas station and there on the corner across the street is the Quick Mart.

It looks almost like it did on the news and in the papers, but there's no police tape, no cruisers, no shattered glass. Nothing on the ground to show what might have happened. It's all perfectly normal and, because of what he knows but cannot see, perfectly grotesque at the same time.

How long does he stand there? Five minutes? Fifteen? He can't remember afterwards.

He uses the extra bus ticket from Friday to get home. At the apartment, his dinner is on the table and Cleo's watching TV. His mother's fallen asleep on the couch.

By the time she wakes up, he's doing his homework in front of the screen as if he's been home for hours, and she doesn't ask where he's been.

11

Dear Amy,

I'm not going to write about what's happening at home any more. I've told you too much already, things you don't need to know. That's not what I was going to tell you about anyway. I was going to tell you about school, things you'd be interested in, things you'd want to know.

There are 357 holes in each of the roof panels in the grade nine room. I'm telling you that because you like to count things—railway cars, street lights, the leaves on the tree at Third Bend.

Do you remember the afternoon at Third Bend? It was the best. The best. I'd never played hooky before. I'd never done anything that I wasn't supposed to do.

Remember how the principal almost caught us the first time? He was driving in late from lunch and stopped his car to ask why we were heading across the park when the bell was about to ring. "But it's just half past twelve!" The way you said it, even I thought your watch had stopped. And it made the next time we tried it all the more daring.

It was the next week, hot and sunny and way too nice for kids to be in school anyway. We left right at the noon bell and used the back alleys. You knew the place to go, down to the park along the river and then up a little creek past the canoe rentals. It even had a name, Third Bend.

We were the only ones there. The grass was as high as our knees and the water laughed and there were grasshoppers and minnows and frogs. And there was just us, sitting on the bank with our feet in the water, lying back in the grass and looking up at the tree and the counting leaves. I didn't even know there was a place like that in the city.

It was the best day. The best.

Nowadays the only things to count are the holes in the roof panels of the grade nine room when I go to French class.

What I want to know is this, why is it so boring to learn French? It would be great to be able to speak French, but the learning is soooo boring you think you're going to die right there. It's like Chinese water torture—the same little droplet hitting you over and over. *Je suis. Tu es. Il est. Elle est.* And the French teacher tries so hard it's enough to drive you nuts. You can almost feel his neurons racing around in frantic bursts of energy. *Je suis! Tu es! Il est! Elle est!* It tires me out watching him. It tires everyone out. The class stumbles out of French like a bunch of zombies.

Did I tell you about our own teacher, Ms. Helpful, the one who smiles a lot? Her neurons don't race around. In fact, she's kind of calm. It's the sort of calmness that is like a mask. She used to be a beauty pageant queen. I'm not kidding. She was Miss Harvest Festival a couple of years ago, and they must have given her lots of clothes or something because she's worn a different outfit every day since I started school. In three weeks she's never worn the same thing twice, and it all matches—shoes, skirt, purse, lipstick. Weird. But then who am I to talk? I'm the kid who wore a dress on the first day of school.

I'm still hanging around with the kids I met that first day, Carolyn and Jade and Ellie, but not all at once because they're different from each other and don't exactly get along. They trade me off between them, the new kid, the one they feel sorry for, at least Carolyn and Jade. Ellie's so quiet I'm not sure how she feels about me. For my part I feel like an apple being sorted for size, and shape, and colour. At least I haven't been tossed out yet.

Once in a while I hang out with Twyla at school, too. Usually that's when she talks Jade and me into following the boys around, the grade nine boys. It's pretty weird. They know we're following them, and we know they know we're following them, but everyone pretends it's just accidental when we end up in the same places, behind the groundkeeper's building or at the far side of the parking lot where the little kids don't go.

I don't know why I go along. I can't talk to anyone when we do meet up. Twyla and Jade can. Twyla knows them all from class and from living here forever, and Jade, well the way all the boys in our class are in love with her. I guess it's not surprising that the older boys like her too, but I just clam up.

I've gotten to know some of the boys in my own class though, and talking to them is OK. Jason, who sits across the aisle, is easy to talk to. He comes up to about my shoulder and he draws great pictures. Travis is easy to talk to. He lives on a cattle ranch and wears cowboy boots all the time. He likes to kid me about being a city kid, but he does it nicely so I don't mind. Norm is easy to talk to, except none of the girls do unless they absolutely have to. I don't know why some people fit and some people don't, even in a little place like this.

But there's one boy in our class that I can't talk to. You guessed it, Ryland. I mean I can talk to him, but I sound weird. Every time I open my mouth around him I say something stupid.

It's his fault. If he'd just be like the others, I'd be OK. I mean he is like the others, everyone likes him and he's good at sports, which always helps, but he's outside everyone else too, thinking things, trying to figure things out.

You want to know something crazy? Sometimes I sit in class and think of things in my head that I might say to him, really deep things like "hi" and "yes" and "did you get your math homework done?" But I don't say them. I can't. I don't think I've spoken more than three words to him since I got here.

But sometimes when I turn around, he's looking at me.

12

"I'm open. Here! Here!"

He's glad he signed up for house leagues. Burning up and down the gym floor at noon is much better than hanging around the halls, and now there's usually something to joke about with the kids in class afterwards. On days when they don't have leagues, a bunch of them eat together in the lunch room.

In Woodworking, the teacher has spent hours hammering all the rules of the shop into their heads, made sure they all know how to use the equipment safely, made sure they understand how important it is not to mess around with anything. There are only a few basic machines they'll be allowed to use this first term, and only when the teacher is standing beside them, but that's better than nothing and Sam's glad they aren't being treated completely like four-year-olds.

They're at the point where they can choose a project. He decides on a wooden airplane with moving wheels and propeller. It looks good in the picture, even if it isn't made to fly. It's the kind of project you do to learn about wood—some basic cutting, a hole or two to drill, and then a lot of hand sanding and finishing.

"Quite a bit of work considering we don't go much later than January with this class," says the shop teacher. "But if that's what you want to try, go for it."

It's not the limited amount of class time that's the problem. Chalmers and his gang messing around is what holds things up. Sam spends an entire period thinking he's lost the plans until someone finds them stuck with chewing gum to the back wall. He loses another day because it's Chalmers' first time on the band saw and even with the teacher standing on top of him, he finds a way to grandstand. Every moment's good for a laugh of some kind when Chalmers is around.

Maybe it doesn't matter. Things are going OK in his other classes. Maybe, for this class, he doesn't have to care.

13

Dear Amy,

I saw Josh today.

It was awful Amy. I went over to Carolyn's for a sleep-over. I couldn't figure out how to say no without hurting her feelings.

We rode home together on her bus. Carolyn sits at the front, right behind the driver. She says good-bye to the little kids as they get off and reminds them if they forget their backpacks. Carolyn's a lot different from Twyla.

Her farm is near the end of the route. There's a great red barn, like in kindergarten picture books, and it's surrounded by granaries and farm equipment and cattle. Her cat met us at the end of her drive and trotted beside us as we walked up the lane. I never knew cats did things like that.

The house is an old, two-storey farmhouse. Carolyn has a room way at the top with a gabled window, the kind I always wanted. There are posters, stuffed animals, mobiles, books, souvenirs, tapes, CDs, photos and a million other things crammed in every corner. Years of living in the same room. My room used to be like that.

We were down having snacks when her mom and sister got home from Winosa, which is a town halfway to the city. Her mom works part-time at the Health Unit there and her sister goes to the high school. They're both pretty nice in an ordinary kind of way. They have thick, curly hair and glasses, which maybe explains why Carolyn keeps talking about contacts and a haircut. Carolyn told her sister that she and I were going to watch a movie tonight so the TV room was booked.

Carolyn's job is to collect the eggs. I'd never done that before. It's kind of like hunting for Easter eggs, because the hens try to hide them. Carolyn showed me how and where to reach under the straw and once we reached right under a hen, the feathers softer than you would believe and warm, warm. When we finished, it was time for supper.

"Is that a car I hear, Mother?"

Carolyn's dad is a great big man who wears coveralls and talks in that old-fashioned way. We'd just sat down to supper and he was trying to see out the window, but there are a lot of trees around the house. Pretty soon, however, we heard footsteps and someone's voice talking to the cat.

I saw a figure on the other side of the screen door, a figure in blue jeans and a light shirt and just the right height and just the right weight and the right way of standing and I knew who it was. I knew. And it felt like my heart was going to explode.

Josh. I think I even said his name. Josh.

But it wasn't. Of course it wasn't. Even as I said it, Carolyn's mom had pushed back from the table and was hurrying to the door. Carolyn's father was grinning and saying "Well, well, well!"

It was Carolyn's brother. I didn't even know she had one. They weren't expecting him. Carolyn's mom and dad were so pleased they just shone. Dale (that's his name) was pretty pleased himself. He hugged his mom and shook hands with his dad and called Carolyn "Small Fry". He began to crack jokes with his older sister and without missing a beat, she began to crack jokes right back.

It was the strangest feeling, Amy. Everyone else around the table, Dale and his mom and his dad and his older sister especially, were all laughing and joking, and I felt like the whole world had dropped out from under me. I couldn't eat. I couldn't move. I felt like I was clinging to a ledge in space and if I let go even for an instant I'd fall.

I don't know if anyone noticed. They were all so busy making a fuss over him that I don't think they did. Another plate was set and everyone began to talk, especially everyone who was older. Pretty soon Carolyn excused us and we went into the TV room.

We were just starting to watch the movie when her mom came in.

"Carolyn, there's a hockey game tonight. You know how much Dale and your dad like to watch hockey together. Could you two girls use the little TV in our room instead?"

Carolyn unhooked the DVD player and carried it into the back bedroom, but there was a storm cloud over her head. As soon as she closed the sewing room door, she scowled.

"Dale always hogs the TV. He hogs everything. And he always calls me Small Fry like I'm a little kid. I hate him."

I lost it, Amy. I just lost it.

"Don't you ever say that!" The words exploded out of me. I couldn't have stopped them if I'd wanted to. I was practically spitting them, I was so mad. "Don't you ever say you hate your brother or your sister or anyone else. I mean it. Don't you ever say that again!"

Carolyn's face went splotchy, but what could she say?

Her sleepover friend had turned into a raving lunatic, and she didn't understand why. But I wasn't going to apologize. No way was I going to apologize.

We turned on the movie, but we didn't talk at all. Halfway through I said I was feeling sick and needed to go home.

That's where I am now, at home in my bedroom with clothes pushed against the crack at the bottom of the door so Mom and Dad won't know I've still got the light on.

She just didn't know how lucky she was, Amy. They're all so lucky and they have no idea how much it matters, even her mom and dad and sister who were so glad to see Dale, even they didn't really know. They should know! They shouldn't just take it for granted! But there's something else too, something I don't even like to admit.

I'm jealous, Amy. They're still a family. Why them? Why not us too? We weren't horrible people. We were just us. Just a family.

I'm so jealous I want to throw something and scream and hit someone. I don't even like being jealous, but it's how I feel.

And there's something else. Layers and layers of something else. There were times when Josh and I didn't get along. Sometimes I was even like Carolyn. I said stupid things. I didn't know. I didn't mean it. I didn't understand.

I'm not sorry I got mad at Carolyn for what she said, but how am I going to face her at school on Monday? What if she tells everyone else about it?

The new kid is crazy.

The new kid is crazy.

The new kid is crazy.

Oh, Amy. What have I done?

14

It's one of the good days.

In floor hockey, he scores not just one goal, but two.

In Woodworking, Chalmers doesn't show up for class. Sam gets a chance to really work on his airplane, gets to use the band saw to cut out the basic shapes. Even though it's done from a pattern, there's something magical about seeing the shapes grow out of the wood. He begins to get more interested than he thought he would.

In Math he figures out a way to calculate the height of the tree. It's not the method the teacher was looking for, but it works and the teacher lets him out of class fifteen minutes early. It means he's got time to walk home and save the bus ticket. He does that on Fridays anyway, when it's early out. Hélène buys the tickets from him. She lives just at the edge of the bus limit and on days when she doesn't want to walk she has to pay her own way. He's learned to leave the English "h" sound off the front of her name and pronounce the é and è sounds too—well, almost. She doesn't ask him to give her a deal on the tickets.

It's only when he gets home that things change. His mom and Cleo are out. It doesn't make sense because he knows his mom has to go to work soon. He's looking for a note when the door opens and they both come in.

Cleo has a two-scoop ice cream cone. His mom has rented her a movie, too, and she slides it into the player, switches on the TV. It's the movie Cleo has been asking to see for a long time. She settles down to watch as Sam follows his mom to the kitchen.

"Some kid at school was giving her the gears about Everett," his mom says, looking out the window. "She came home crying."

She turns to look at him.

"What do I do? Do I phone the school? Does that make it worse? Or better? She's seven years old, for crying out loud. Why can't they just leave her alone. Why can't they leave all of us alone?"

He shakes his head. He doesn't have any answers.

"I'll wait a few days," she says. "See how it goes. But if I have to phone the school I will. It's not fair."

15

Dear Amy,

I was feeling pretty bad Friday night. I guess you knew that. Saturday wasn't wonderful either. I had trouble just getting out of bed and I watched TV all day. That's one way to turn off your brain I guess.

This morning, to keep myself from thinking about things, I went out and helped Dad with the chores in the barn again. It didn't help a lot. Dad was pretty down. I'm not sure he even realized I was there. I was walking back to the house when a horse and rider came up the lane and into the yard.

It was a big horse, big and black as licorice, with two white socks, and whoever was riding it was sitting upright and completely at ease without a saddle, just the horse and the rider looking so comfortable together that I didn't even think of them as being separate. I didn't think that I might know one of them until she raised a hand and called hello.

It was Ellie. She's phoned me every weekend to see if I wanted to go riding. I've always made some sort of excuse. Today she didn't phone. She just arrived.

"I couldn't stop him!" she said. "He just headed down to your place. There are lots of great places to ride, but Nibs gets tired of going on his own. I guess that's why he came here."

It wasn't hard to figure out that Nibs was her big black horse, but it took me another moment to be really, really sure it was Ellie. She seemed so… well, happy is the only word I can think of. She was just happy sitting on top of this great, huge horse that seemed to move like water beneath her. She wasn't invisible any more either.

Before I knew it she and I were riding up the big hill.

Nelson liked being out of the little pasture. He seemed to wake up, or maybe it was having another horse around that did it. I didn't have to keep pulling his head out of the grass, in fact he didn't stop to eat at all, and as we reached the top of the hill and the wind came whistling across to greet us, I could feel a wonderful energy building around us.

Nibs' ears went forward and his legs began to dance. Ellie grinned across at me.

"Are you ready?" she asked.

Ready for what? Before I had time to ask, however, she'd leaned forward and Nibs, in some way I can't explain, had come up to meet her so that they were gathered together into one single living body that was like a spring, coiled and ready to be released.

"Let's go!" called Ellie and she and Nibs took off at a mad gallop across the field.

Nelson took off too. I never knew he had it in him. One minute he was just Nelson and the next moment I was sitting on an explosion. Before I could even think to try and rein him in, he was racing after Nibs and Ellie as hard as he could go.

For one glorious, terrifying second I was part of it all! And then I fell off.

I've never fallen as hard as that. Every breath of air was smacked right out of my body. I could feel my heart thumping like crazy out of sheer fear and my nerve endings were all running around saying "Are you crazy? Are you trying to kill yourself? Are you crazy?"

Then I heard a real voice.

"Kate? Are you OK? I'm really sorry. I thought you could ride. I really did."

That was Ellie. She was kneeling beside me and Nelson and Nibs were there too. They were standing looking at me like I was some sort of pathetic creature, and Nelson even swung his big head down over mine and snorted horse breath on me.

I got back on. Not right away, I had to wait for the world to stop spinning and get my breath, but when things had settled a bit, I asked Ellie to boost me back on Nelson.

"We'll go slow," said Ellie.

"No way," I told her. "Yaahhhhh!"

Once again the horses took off. Once again I was lying on the ground.

This time when Ellie boosted me back on, she was just plain mad. She wouldn't let go of Nelson's reins.

"I don't care if you kill yourself," she said, "but you're going to ruin a perfectly good horse if you keep this up, so listen to me. Lean forward. Hug with your knees. And hold onto Nelson's mane for dear life."

So that's what I did.

I've galloped a couple of times in a saddle on Mr. Limster's dude horses in Banff, but it's nothing like galloping bareback on horses that really want to run. Galloping bareback you do exactly what Ellie says. You lean forward and hug with your knees and try to make yourself part of the horse. And the horse just moves. It just moves beneath you with its big muscles pulling and pulling and eating up the ground.

I fell off two more times stopping. Stopping is harder than you'd think, except by that time I was getting my balance so I kind of slid off and didn't get really hurt. And I almost got joggled to death trotting.

But galloping along the top of the big hill is like galloping along the top of the world. I would have galloped all the way home but Ellie warned me not to gallop downhill or Nelson might hurt himself. Going downhill, you lean back and let the horse take his time. Going uphill, you lean forward to help the horse. But on the flat parts you can let something else take over. You can gallop like crazy.

I have bruises all up and down my right side and my legs ache, but I'm not telling Mom and Dad. I'm not telling them about the bruises. I'm not telling them about Nelson the Wonder Horse.

You're the only one I'm telling. You're the only one who'd understand.

And next chance I get I'm going riding with Ellie again.

16

"Ten minutes. Otherwise maybe I'll call someone else."

It's Saturday and Chalmers has phoned to say he's got his hands on the latest video game, the one everyone's talking about. Sam knows without asking that Chalmers has already played non-stop since Friday night so he's sure he can trample Sam. That's how Chalmers operates. Sam agrees to go over anyway.

The address Chalmers gives is uphill along the number 18 bus route, which is why he ended up at Winston Jr. High, Sam guesses. As he heads out, Sam tells himself he'll turn around and come home if there's other stuff going on, if it's not just video games. There's stuff Chalmers gets into that Sam doesn't want to go near, but he thinks it's just the game. Still, as he starts up the hill he tries to think of excuses for why he said yes on the phone in the first place.

Excuse number one: when he picked up the phone he didn't expect it to be Chalmers.

Excuse number two: it's a good chance to figure out what Chalmers wants.

Excuse number three: Chalmers isn't so bad on his own, when he doesn't have his followers to impress.

Or maybe, Sam thinks, he's more lonely than he wants to admit.

They play for eight hours solid. It's later than he thought by the time he leaves and when he gets home his mom's plenty worried. He didn't tell her where he was going.

"I was with a kid I know from school. We weren't getting into trouble," he says. "We were just playing video games."

He doesn't say which kid. When they lived across the hall, there was more than one time when the cops visited the apartment where Chalmers and his family lived. His mom knows that.

"You have to phone," she says. "You have to phone and tell me what's going on so I don't worry. You can understand that I'd worry. You can understand that much, right? That's how it started, with your brother. He'd go out and I'd never know where he was going or when he'd be back."

No, thinks Sam. That wasn't how it started. It started way before that.

The idea takes him by surprise. How does he know that? Why is he so certain?

And suddenly, scattered scraps and pieces from the past begin to rise. Things he'd allowed to fall out of memory.

A snapped wheel on a toy truck that may or may not have been an accident. A wrestling hold that was a little too rough. A deck of cards found singed and crumpled in the garbage after Everett hadn't won the game.

That's just the way older brothers are, he'd thought. How could he have known any different? What did he have to compare things to?

But those aren't the things he tells his mom. However it started, she's right about it playing out that way—Everett not coming home when he was expected and then suddenly being there, slipping into the apartment, breathing hard and looking out the window as if someone might be following him, locking himself in the bedroom as if none of them existed. Either that or flying into a rage if someone even looked at him like he should explain.

How could he worry his mom like this?

"I'll call next time," he says. "I promise."

The part that scares him, however, is that he knows he's lying. If he hangs out with Chalmers again, he won't be calling. You can't tell someone like Chalmers that you have to phone your mom.

17

Dear Amy,

This is the way the dream goes.

We're at the skating rink, you and I, way up high where we like to sit. It's a hockey game. We don't know the score. We never do. We join in the cheering when it's for our team because Josh is playing, but really we're just there because it's a good chance to hang out together.

The third period is about to begin. The Zamboni is going off the ice and behind it the surface is smooth as glass. And then, like glass, it cracks. It cracks right across like a mirror. And then again. And then again

I realize it's cracking because someone is shooting at it, shooting in bursts, like from a machine gun in a TV show. And it's not like a mirror cracking now, it's like window glass, a window shattering, shattering into thousands of pieces.

I look up and see it's Josh who is shooting. Josh is up in the stands and he's wearing a pair of Mom's gardening gloves to keep his hands clean and he's shooting.

"Cut it out!" I yell. "Cut it out!"

He doesn't hear me. He shoots again. I look at the rink. There's shattered glass everywhere, shattered glass and candy, sours and jujubes and cinnamon hearts, except they aren't cinnamon hearts at all, they're drops of blood. It's awful. Awful. I don't want to look but I can't make myself turn away. I look and I look and I look.

And then I think , this can't be happening. Josh wouldn't

do something like that. And then my mind gives another little click and remembers. Josh couldn't do something like that. Josh isn't alive any more. And that's when I wake up.

Waking up is almost as bad as the dream itself.

I don't know if I should have told you.

I don't know if I should have written it down.

But now, even if I dream it again, I can tell myself I don't have to remember. I don't have to relive it all over when I'm awake as well as when I'm asleep. It doesn't need me to remember it. It's written down.

I'm sorry.

I'm sorry.

I'm sorry.

18

"One, two, buckle my shoe,
  Three, four, shut the door."

They've been out shopping and Cleo is swinging the bag with her brand new shoes, singing to herself as the elevator rattles its way up to the fourth floor of their building.

"Five, six, pick up sticks."

The elevator jolts to a stop. The door slides open. Down the corridor, the lady in 410 is just coming out of her apartment when she glances up and sees them. She turns, goes back into her apartment and closes the door rather than pass them in the hall.

"Seven, eight, lay them straight…" prompts their mother as they step from the elevator…

But Cleo doesn't join in.

"We could move," he tells his mom after Cleo has gone to bed.

She shakes her head.

"If I'd thought that would solve anything, we'd have done it a long time ago," she says.

He knows from experience that when Cleo goes to put on her shoes tomorrow, they won't feel quite as fresh and new.

19

Dear Amy,

Sometimes, when I'm at school, its like time skips a beat. I get lost in the gap for a long time, and then I wake up and discover things have been happening.

Do you remember how I was worried about seeing Carolyn at school after what happened at the sleepover? I thought she'd think I was crazy and stay away from me. Well it didn't work like that.

Instead of staying away she's adopted me full time. She's always hovering around me, asking me if I feel OK, making sure I'm her partner for projects in class, and hanging out with me at recess and noon hour. Today she dragged me into a baseball game she wanted to organize.

Baseball. Crazy eh? You know how bad I am at baseball. Remember all those games we played with John Keily and his friends? They only let us play because you were good at it—good enough for both of us to play—that's how good you were.

Carolyn's baseball game was a lot more organized. There were teams and rules. Lots of kids played, including Ryland and Travis and Norm. Carolyn made herself one of the captains, so I was picked first and I chose second base. There's not much action at second base. All I had to worry about was being up at bat and I knew I always strike out or hit some sort of feeble thing the pitcher catches bare-hand. I knew what to expect.

Except that's not what happened. When it was my turn

to bat, Ryland came up to me. He was on our team and I thought he was going to tell me all those dumb things gym teachers say, keep your eye on the ball, choke up the bat, but he didn't.

"There's a big hole in left field," he said.

There was too. Norm was visiting at third instead of covering short stop, and Ellie was out in field sitting cross-legged in the grass and dreaming about galloping a million miles an hour on Nibs.

I hit the ball right through the hole.

"Run! Run!" That's what everyone began shouting. "Run!"

I ran. I ran all the way to first and across second and touched third and across home plate and across the playground and back to the school and down to the washroom and locked myself in one of the cubicles.

All of a sudden I just needed to be alone.

Bathroom cubicles aren't the nicest places, but after a while you get used to them. You can think about things in bathroom cubicles.

I thought about Ellie out in left field dreaming. I haven't talked to her since we went riding. I've had lots of chances, but when I see her I feel like I don't know who she is. I feel like I don't know who I am either. It's hard to explain.

I thought about Ryland noticing the hole in left field. He just assumed I could hit the ball in that direction. I never even knew you could control where the ball went unless you were some kind of big league star.

I thought about the feeling I get sometimes, the feeling that makes me hide in bathroom cubicles. I get scared.

Panicky scared. Stupid scared. Scared the school bus won't stop for me. Scared I'll come home from school and a tornado will have hit the farm and no one will be here. Scared I'll actually hit the ball and the world will fall apart.

I'm not supposed to be able to hit the ball.

Now that I'm home in my bedroom, I know it was just one of those things, one of those times when my mind and my body decided to work together. It doesn't happen very often but that's all it was. I didn't need to feel like the world was coming to an end. I didn't need to hide.

It's a good thing a lot of kids believed my stomachache story because it made it easier to use this time.

Except I know Jade didn't believe it. And Ryland probably thinks I'm nuts.

20

"Come in everyone," says the lady who opens the door. "I've cleared off the big table downstairs in case you need it."

They've had weeks to finish their science project, but it's still not done. One of the kids in the group, the one who lives close to the school, invites the three of them over after class so they can finish it in on time.

The house is big and has a basement where they can lay everything out. It's clear from the moment his mom opens the door that she's the kind from the little-kid movies. She brings them chips and dips, offers them coloured macaroni for their project, even though the projects you do in junior high aren't the macaroni and glue kind. It's the computer beside the big table that they're mostly going to use.

"I don't think I've met you before, Sam," she says. "Do you live around here?"

"Not as close to the school as this," he answers.

"What do your parents do?"

"They work downtown," he answers.

"Maybe I'll meet them at parent council," she says. "Do you have any brothers and sisters?"

"Not at Winston," he answers.

He can tell the mom likes him, thinks he'd be a good friend for her son.

"You'll have to come over again, Sam," she says. "Do you think it would be OK with your folks?"

"I think so," he says. "I'll ask to be sure."

His answers have all been either true, half-true, or

could-be-true. His dad could be working in some downtown, somewhere. He will let his mom know where he's going if he gets invited over.

But part of him feels sick. Everett was good at this kind of thing, good at getting people to believe in almost anything. The effortless telling lies and half lies—that's another way it played out with Everett.

But still not the way it started.

How did it start? Would it help to remember? Would he be able to tell for certain it wasn't happening to him too?

"Have some more chips," says the mom.

21

Dear Amy,

Dad and Mom have had a fight, not just the little ones they've been having lately, a big one.

I don't understand. Is there just so much good luck in life and then that's it? When you use up your share of happiness does everything just fall apart? Or are there things I don't know, things you have to do, special small things, like the way you walk or sit or speak, to keep the bad things from happening? When I was little I used to fold the top sheet on my bed in an extra-wide band over the blanket. It kept the monsters away. I've started doing it again.

Sometimes I sit and try to think of all the things that happened the evening before the Quick Mart. I look for signs that something was going to happen. I try to remember if there were crows, or black cats, or wild weather, or shadows, or the feeling of something dark nearby. There wasn't. There were only little things, good things. The lady across the street won two hundred dollars at bingo. You and I found our favourite playing piece, the shoe, for the Monopoly game.

I don't play Monopoly anymore. Ever.

It was because of Aunt Stella's boyfriend that Mom and Dad had the fight. Mike, that's his name, Mike. They came out yesterday. I took him down to the riding ring as soon as they arrived because that's what he asked me to do. Mom and Aunt Stella were headed into the house for one of Aunt Stella's marathon talking sessions.

We saw a movie in science about animal behaviour last week, greeting rituals among baboons. I never noticed it before, but people have greeting rituals too. Dad was working the grey gelding named Acer. He knew we were coming, but he didn't stop right away. He rode an extra loop at the far side of the ring, stopped, had Acer back up eight paces, and then turned the gelding toward us in an even, flat-footed walk, while looking calmly out from beneath his cowboy hat. That's Dad's greeting ritual. Nice and slow. Not unfriendly, but not giving anything away either.

Stella's boyfriend went into a greeting ritual of his own. He shifted from one foot to the other, pulled himself upright, ran his hand over his hair, gave the change in his pocket a shake and smiled in a large sort of way. When Dad was close enough, he held out his hand and introduced himself. It's a good thing he did too, because I'd forgotten his name.

They talked about horses for a minute or two. It sounded like Mike knew a bit about them. After that Dad went back to riding and Mike and I watched.

Mike's the kind of person who likes to talk about what he knows. He told me about things I'd seen Dad do, but hadn't exactly understood. He pointed out how smoothly Dad had Acer change from a walk to a canter without that bumping jog Nelson sometimes likes to put in. He explained how Acer's inside front leg always reached out ahead, how he was always on the inside lead when he cantered around the ring. It's the inside leg because that makes the most sense for turning and that's the one Dad asks Acer to lead with, using a touch of one leg and a pull so light it can't even be seen on the opposite rein. I didn't even know what a lead was, but it all made sense once Mike pointed it out.

When Mike got tired of watching and headed up to the house, I felt like trying it out on Nelson. By the time I reached the pasture, however, reality had set in. I couldn't go down to the ring and try things with Dad working Acer there. If I went up over the hill, all Nelson was going to want to do was run like Ellie and I had done.

So I did the opposite. I rode Nelson wild and free. No bridle. Not even a halter or a piece of rope. I just went out into the pasture and found a rock to stand on and swung aboard. It felt kind of daring, except of course it wasn't because when Nelson's in the little pasture, he doesn't do anything except walk around eating grass and being happy.

But I did something really dumb afterward. On the way back to the house, I decided to play Indian scout sneaking up on the enemy. Don't ask me why I did it. I guess it was the no-bridle thing. Or maybe too much TV.

Anyway, I ran back and forth across the yard between the barn and the house, running from hiding place to hiding place, thinking I was being really sneaky. I even thought I was getting away with it , until I got close enough to see them standing in the living room window. Mom and Aunt Stella and Mike were standing at the living room window watching me. I'm pretty sure they were laughing.

Why do I do stupid things like that?

Why couldn't they just ignore me!

I spent the rest of the day locked in my bedroom reading a book Twyla gave me. Well, I wasn't really locked in, my door doesn't have a lock, but I closed it good and tight so people would know I didn't want company.

It was a very interesting book about sex, very interesting. Her sister gave it to her. You could tell by the bent pages that some parts had been read a lot more than others. At least now I know why Twyla says I'm pretty dumb for a city kid.

I was still in my room when Stella and Mike left, and that's when Mom and Dad had the fight. It was because Dad didn't come into the house while Mike was here.

"You could have tried," Mom said. "Stella brought him out especially because she thought he was someone you could talk to."

"Talk about what? Horses? Some high-priced lawyer whose daughter puddled in pony club and now he thinks he's an expert?"

"You could have tried talking about other things. He knew about things. He knew about Josh."

"Was that Stella's idea too?"

When Mom and Dad fight, they don't fight loud, but the sound of their voices changes. It becomes clear and tight, even if you can't hear what they're saying. And just about the time you feel the tightness is going to snap, one of them leaves. It was Mom this time. She went down to the studio and slammed the door.

I don't even know why I'm telling you about them fighting except it makes me feel better to talk to you, it makes me feel better, that is, until I get to thinking that someone in your family might be doing the same thing. Fighting. Slamming doors. Not your mom and dad, I don't think you ever even knew where your dad lived, but your Mom and somebody else, somebody like your grandmother, the one in the photograph with the great, round glasses that made her look like an owl so that you used to open your eyes enormous and round and say "Do you think I'll grow up to look like her?"

When I think of something like that, I almost want to give up.

But I can't.

You wouldn't have.

22

His mother's been in bed all weekend. She says it's the flu. It's not. One of her friends shows up at the door, a friend who's been around for twenty years, who was around when Everett was born.

"Your mom phoned me," she says. "I think I need to be here."

She goes into the bedroom and they talk a long time. He takes Cleo to the park so she won't hear their mother crying.

He pushes Cleo higher and higher on the swing. She laughs and shouts happily. Higher and higher he pushes her.

"Give me an under-duck!" she cries.

The memory hits him with a swiftness he could not have imagined—engulfs him with leaf smell, shriek of metal, rush of wind. Everett, taking him to the park, pushing him higher and higher. Only Sam hadn't liked to go high. He can remember the feel of the chain in his hands as he clung on for dear life. He can remember begging Everett to let him come down.

"You haven't had the best part yet, Sammy," Everett had said instead. "Under-duck time."

But he hadn't done it right away. He'd waited. One push. Two pushes. And then a hard, high, lurching jolt.

Sam grabs the plastic that is Cleo's swing seat and eases her to a stop.

"We have to go," he says. "We'll walk by the lake and see the ducks."

He sees his mother and her friend crossing the street on the far side of the park. They're walking towards the cemetery. Nothing makes any sense any more.

23

Dear Amy,

If I couldn't write to you, I'm not sure what would happen. Time moves in uneven heartbeats, and I drop into the gaps. Then something happens and I think "Amy would be interested in that," and somehow I find myself here on my bed writing to you and I feel almost real again.

Ellie finally cornered me at school and asked me if I was mad at her. I did the best I could. It told her she's like two people, the person at school, and the person who rides Nibs. That made her laugh.

"Which person do you like best?" she asked.

"They're both OK," I said. "They're just different."

"I like the person that rides Nibs better," she said, and laughed again. When she laughs she's not quite as invisible, even in class. I think she'll ride down again soon.

Twyla and Jade have been dragging me off to follow the grade nine boys again. I think Carolyn would be miffed with me, except Ms. Helpful has asked her to help organize the library. I'm not very good at library organization, but I'm great at coming back later and listening to what she's done, so she doesn't mind much when I take off with Twyla and Jade.

Actually we're not exactly following the boys any more. Twyla has a new plan. Her sister gave her a portable CD player for her birthday and she brings it to school now. On nice days, and with the leaves turned golden the days have gotten nice again—crispness and sunshine all at once—we sit out on the lawn near the parking lot and listen to CDs. Most of the time the grade nine boys drift over and listen too.

It's easier for me with the CD player. If I don't know what else to do (which is ninety percent of the time) I can pretend I'm listening to the music.

Jason, Travis, and Ryland come by sometimes too. When that happens Twyla usually wanders away, she's not very interested in boys younger than her. And we have a special sign that means Norm is headed our way so we can all pack up real quick. I guess that's kind of mean, but it's not as bad as the way some of the grade nine girls call him over and then tease him. It's not nice teasing either.

I don't see the older girls much, but I hear about them from Twyla in the back of the bus.

"Becky was in a real snit today because someone drew cartoons on her science book."

"All Claire does is study so she can show everyone up on math tests."

"Annie tried to dye her hair red but it turned orange, so now she's pretending that's the colour she really wanted. She's such a fake."

Twyla's class is even smaller than our grade, so I guess it's hard for her to find someone she gets along with. Jade and I are it.

Yesterday, Twyla asked me to get off the bus and stay at her place for supper. The bus driver waited while we phoned my mom. I was afraid she'd be in the studio and wouldn't answer, but she did. Maybe she's got a phone down there now.

Twyla's mom and dad are older, almost like grandparents. Her dad isn't very healthy, so Twyla helps a lot with the chores. She doesn't just collect the eggs, she brings the cows in from the fields and helps her dad feed and milk them, and feeds her own 4-H Club calf. It's kind of weird seeing someone with spiked hair and black eye liner wading through the barnyard muck to pitch hay over the fence to a red-and-white steer.

"I only belong to 4-H Club because I get to keep the money when I sell my steer," she told me. "It's not like there's any place you can get a job around here.

We spent a lot of time doing chores and then we ate and helped with the dishes, so it was already after eight by the time we got to hang out in Twyla's room and listen to CDs.

Twyla's mom likes doilies and frills and china figurines in her part of the house. Twyla's own room is a different world entirely. She has black curtains and a shiny bedspread that glows eerily when she turns on the purple bulb in the lamp on her desk. The walls are tacked all over with pictures from music and movie magazines. Her sister gets her the magazines.

"One day I'm going to move to the city and live with my sister," she told me. "You can come too."

One days don't happen.

Twyla has a black pillowcase. She sewed it herself from the same material she used to make the curtains. She says it's great because her eyeliner doesn't show if she forgets to wash it off at night.

I'm still not sure about Twyla.

24

He wakes up sweating. It's been happening since the day his mother said "that's how it started"—images rising that he can push away when he's awake but that come at night, unwanted, determined. Nightmare jumbles. They've become worse since the day at the park with Cleo. Everett's swiftly changing moods. Things thrown, broken, smashed. Or just the ever-present threat of things going off the rails.

He climbs out of bed, goes into the hall. He's looking for something. He doesn't know what.

Quietly he stands in the darkness. Listening. Peering. Waiting. Suddenly he knows what he's looking for. He's looking to see if Everett is prowling through the house. Not the apartment, the house. They lived in a house before things began to fall apart. Everett used to wake up and wander through the rooms. Not hurting anything, not bothering anyone, but restless, prowling.

Sam couldn't have named it at the time, but looking back he sees that he must have felt it even then. Something dark on the horizon. Storm approaching.

If his mom wants to talk about when it started, that's the spot that Sam remembers.

He goes to bed before he can find himself prowling too.

25

Dear Amy,

Sometimes when I lie in bed early in the morning, I have a funny feeling. I feel like if I just didn't ever get up, if I just never opened my eyes, everything would be OK. Josh would still be alive, I'd still have a real family, we wouldn't have moved, you'd be living three blocks away, Mom and Dad wouldn't be fighting, and I wouldn't ever have heard what one of the girls from Josh's class said. I was walking home from school and there were three girls from his class on the other side of the street. Two of them said hi to me, I'd seen them with Josh a couple of times and they'd even come by the house afterward. The third girl crossed the street and walked up to me.

"I didn't really like your brother, so it didn't matter to me that he died," she said.

Why did she say that, Amy? How could she think she needed to say that to me? How could she think I needed to hear it?

I don't remember what I said to her. I don't even remember walking the rest of the way home except that when I walked in the door for lunch, Mom asked me what was wrong. I didn't tell her.

It's hard to open your eyes on mornings when you remember things like that. I wouldn't let myself remember it at all until I also remembered that Ellie was coming over to go riding.

"Over the river and through the woods to Grandmother's house we go."

That's what Ellie sang as we cantered along an old vehicle track at the bottom of the big hill. Cantering is almost like galloping except it's slower and smoother, which was good because I wasn't quite as good a rider as I'd remembered. Nibs and Nelson had already had their wild gallop across the top of the big hill and I'd only barely managed to stay on.

"Oops," said Ellie, pulling Nibs to a sudden stop as a grove of trees rose up from the creek. Nelson stopped as well, so I was thrown up on his neck somewhere and had to slide back into place. "I thought it was further along," she said and slid off Nibs beside a gate in the fence.

I'm getting pretty good at opening gates. Most of them take two of us, one to stretch the wires tight and the other to pull the loop over the post. Ellie says people don't mind if we cross their land so long as we always close the gates. And we really were on our way to her grandmother's house.

"It doesn't look like anyone's home," I told her as we rode into a clearing a few minutes later. There were no vehicles in the yard and the tiny cabin had boards over the windows. Ellie shook her head.

"This is the Turlow place. City people," she said. "My dad keeps an eye on things for them. Look, we can see your house from here."

We could, too. Because of the curve of the hill and the open pasture, we could see our farm across the valley. The Turlow place, however, was so well tucked into the woods that I'd never even known it was there.

We followed a dirt lane for a long time after that. Eventually it hooked up with a main road and the land opened up again. We were on a little hill and below us stretched a long, narrow lake, all blue and sunlight and ripples. Farmland was golden on one side and autumn bush was orange and red on the other.

"There's my Gran and Grampa's place," said Ellie, pointing to some buildings close to the water. "It's a lot faster to cut through the way we came than to come around the lake by car."

The wind swept up to us off the lake. The horses began to dance and we galloped full speed across the pasture, racing further than we needed, just to feel them run. We came up to her grandparent's farm by a little hill behind the barn.

That's when I saw something I wish I hadn't. Don't listen if you don't want to. I saw dawn horses.

Do you know what dawn horses are? They're prehistoric horses, small and blunt. They almost look like reptiles in the books, except they aren't reptiles. I think people who draw pictures about prehistoric animals just get so carried away drawing dinosaurs that when they finally get to mammals, everything still looks a bit like a dinosaur.

But there they were on the ground behind the barn, two of them lying motionless on their sides, legs extended straight, as if frozen in stride. Dawn horses. And I remember thinking, how can it be? Can it really be dawn horses?

"Grampa's been shooting coyotes again," said Ellie. "He sells the pelts. Pretty gross, eh?"

Even then I didn't understand right away. My mind had to sort it through, had to see what it didn't want to see. I could almost feel it trying to find some other answer, but there wasn't any.

Death.

That's what it was. Skinned out and lying on the ground, two coyotes shot in the early morning, two blasts from someone's rifle. And Ellie was right, the skinned bodies were gross, naked and reptilian, and obscene.

I wish I hadn't seen them. If we hadn't come up from that side, if we hadn't come on that day, if her grandpa hadn't got up early that morning, or if the coyotes had stayed in the brush along the lake, that would have been best of all, we wouldn't have seen them.

I can't even think about whether or not it's right to shoot coyotes when you're a farmer.

All I can think about is how ugly it was.

Is death always that way? Lying in ambush?

I'm sorry I told you. I'm sorry I saw it. I'm sorry I made you hear.

It was an OK day until then.

26

There's a buzz when he gets to school. He catches snatches of it as he makes his way down the hall, but it's Hélène who fills him in.

"Someone pulled a knife out on the steps after school yesterday," she says.

As soon as they've done homeroom attendance the entire school is called down to the gym for an assembly. It turns out it wasn't on the steps at all. It was a couple of older kids, kids who don't even go to Winston, hanging out across the street, and no one really knows if there was a knife or just something shiny that might have been.

They get the one-hour lecture, of course. No weapons at school. Report anyone hanging around.

But the buzz is still in the hallways when the assembly breaks up. Some girls ahead of him are passing it back and forth between them.

"I bet they did have knives. I bet they just don't want to tell us."

"I heard they had the police in. Searched some of the lockers for drugs."

"My dad says it's not the drug dealers you got to watch out for. It's the psychos, the people that just shoot without even knowing what they're shooting at."

He doesn't turn to look at the girls, but someone just in front of him does. It's the kid from the back of the class, John, only when he turns it's not the girls he's looking at but Sam himself. His face is white and he looks like he's about to be sick.

The girls go sweeping past with the rest of the crowd. Sam lets himself get swallowed and pulled around in its wake.

By the time he gets to Woodworking, he can tell Chalmers has been building the story all day.

"Oh yeah, I know who was hanging around yesterday. They're okay—so long as you don't mess with them."

"Friends of yours?" asks someone.

"Would I have friends like that?" asks Chalmers in mock horror. "Me? I'm an angel. Ask someone who's known me for a long time. Ask Sammy boy."

Eyes slide over to where Sam is working on the blades of the propeller.

"If he says he's an angel that's what he is," says Sam.

"See. Sam here knows me. Come to think of it, Sammy boy, you would have known the guys from yesterday too. They hang around on the corner past the store where I do my "shopping," the store where the clerks aren't so bright. One of the guys has a tattoo on his neck."

Chalmers is right. Sam doesn't know their names, but he knows them by reputation. It wouldn't be surprising for one of them to have a knife.

But he also knows that as much as Chalmers is pretending to have some sort of connection to them, they aren't friends of his either. They're at least three years older and they wouldn't be interested in someone like Chalmers.

At least that's how it used to be. Maybe things have changed. Maybe Chalmers is getting into more than Sam realized.

Sam lifts his shoulders in a guarded shrug. He doesn't want to deny knowing who Chalmers is talking about, doesn't want to admit to it either.

He's going to have to be more careful than he thought.

27

Dear Amy,

Mom and Dad aren't talking to each other. They say the usual things like "I picked up the mail" and "Is this the list of things you want from Winosa?" but they say it extra polite, the way you do with strangers. It makes me want to scream at them, but I'm afraid to. Now I know what people mean by the expression "walking on eggs."

But I try Amy. I've been up until midnight every night this week. That's when Mom comes up from the studio, late, after Dad's already gone to bed. When I hear her footsteps on the stairs from the basement, I take my hot chocolate mug out to the kitchen for a refill.

I keep hoping Mom will tell me what she's working on in the studio, but she doesn't. She just asks me important things like if supper was OK and whether or not I heard the weather forecast. I tell her important things too, like what we're reading in English or how hard the math test was. Those aren't the things I really want to tell her. They aren't the things I really want to ask.

When I go out to the barn with Dad it's the same thing. "Throw a couple of bales of hay down from the loft, Kate," Dad says. More important conversation.

It used to be that sometimes when our parents were acting weird, Josh and I would roll our eyes or make cuckoo signs behind their backs. I can't do that any more. There's only me, Kate, who came second.

More and more it feels like something is about to break.

This weekend, for a little while, it was better. The winter horses arrived late Friday afternoon. Mr. Limster and a friend trucked them in, twenty-eight dude horses that have been used on trail rides all summer. They come in all shapes and sizes, tall, short, dark, light, handsome, homely, kind of like people. The tallest is a great, huge gelding named Sampson who is over seventeen hands tall. "Hands" are how you measure horses, and seventeen hands is big. The smallest is a Shetland pony named Pint-Size Suzy. It's something I've only ever seen in movies, old-time western movies—a whole herd of horses grazing out on the land.

"Ride whichever ones you want," Mr. Limster told Ellie and me, so Saturday morning we took some oats out to the field and caught the two we liked best. They're dude horses all right. They follow one after the other, even where there's plenty of room to ride side by side. They walk very slowly on the way out from the buildings—as if they're sick or something—but once you turn them for home, suddenly they're a whole lot healthier. Ellie thought it was hilarious.

"Let's ride down to the spring," she said. "Maybe they'll wake up after they have a drink of water."

The spring is in the little ravine beyond Nelson's pasture. I'd never been down there before, but I'm going to go again. It's a "just-right" place. The land is fenced so that all three pastures run down to it, the trails zigzagging back and forth so the horses can handle the steep slope on either side. The water seeps out of the canyon walls and gathers in three round wooden troughs nestled at the bottom. It's quiet, just the sunlight through the leaves, a patch of sky overhead, and the water laughing from trough to trough to trough.

The horses were glad to have a drink, but it didn't perk them up any.

"I don't think being on a dude ranch is very good for real horses," said Ellie.

"Maybe they just need a long winter rest," I said.

But I don't really believe it. And Nelson will be a dude horse next year. I didn't tell Ellie that.

While Mr. Limster and his friend were here, Mom cooked up a storm and served meals for all of us together on the dining room table, even breakfast, so that the house smelled warm with bacon and eggs and coffee. Dad and Mr. Limster had the horses and the farm to talk about and Mr. Limster's friend had a million funny stories about taking packhorses and tourists on mountain trails. Mom even told her old story about refusing to ride ever again after getting bucked off into the manure pile a million years ago. Everyone laughed. It was good, or it would have been good if I didn't already know how it was going to be worse than ever after they left.

This morning, Mr. Limster was climbing into his truck when I brought Nelson down from the pasture this morning. He gave me a big wave.

"It looks like you're all doing real fine out here, Kate!" he called.

Mr. Limster's an old friend from my dad's cowboy days. I like him a lot, but he's easy to fool.

28

"It's a good report card," his mom tells him. "Is IA your woodworking class? The teacher's certainly impressed with how hard you're working. And look at this math mark—85 percent is amazing. You're good at math just like… "

She stops, bites her lip. Math was the one subject Everett was good at. Numbers fell into patterns for him, adding, multiplying, doing percentages in his head.

Don't say it, Sam thinks. Please don't say it.

But the unfinished sentence hangs in the air, waiting. It's almost as if the words are some strange animal that needs to be fed. The apartment is so quiet that when the refrigerator cuts in it sounds like a Mack truck roaring through the kitchen and still the rest of the apartment is quiet.

Across the room Cleo lifts her head unconcernedly from the picture she's been colouring and smiles.

"Just like me," she says. "I'm good at math and printing. Miss Winters said so."

Rescued by his little sister.

29

Dear Amy,

It's a lot colder here now. The wind has blown the last of the leaves from the trees, and when Ellie and I go riding the grass is frosty beneath the horses' hooves and the ground is frozen hard. It's a good thing I don't fall off much anymore. I wear Mom's gumboots and a heavy pair of socks because otherwise my feet freeze in my running shoes.

But yesterday Mom and I drove into the city. It was her idea. She said I should come too, because I've outgrown a lot of my clothes and it might be our last chance before winter.

"And we can talk on the way, Kate," she said. "There are things we should talk about. I've meant to, but I haven't. Something I need to tell you."

I looked at her hard.

"Don't worry, it's not about your dad and I. Or Josh. At least not exactly."

When we got in the car, though, she didn't talk at all. She turned up the radio and pretended to be interested in the program that was on, so interested she forgot about talking about things. Maybe you and I know what she needed to tell me, why she finds it so hard, why she has to pretend. Maybe we don't.

It's two hours into the city. On the drive in I thought about the dance Friday night. It was my first real dance, not a community dance with fiddle music and accordions either, a school dance. Some of the grade nine girls organized it and one of them had an older cousin who did a pretty good job as DJ.

I didn't really plan on dancing. I was just going to go and see what went on. After a while Travis started teasing me about being a too-cool city kid, so I pretty much had to dance after all. I danced with Jason too, and I'm glad I did, even though he's much shorter than me. He can do mime stuff. Do you know what I mean? Walking in one place. Moving along a wall with his hands. A kind of a dancing, double take.

Do you want to know something? I'd forgotten it until the night of the dance but Josh used to do stuff like that, mime stuff, moon-walking. I don't know if he did it when he was at dances, but he used to do it outside my bedroom door when I was little and was angry about having to go to bed so early. He used to sneak upstairs and entertain me with little tricks. Superman flying across the doorway with a tea-towel cape. A sticky monster climbing the door frame with its sticky, sticky hands. Moon-walking. Wall-walking. He seemed big and wonderful; he must have been about my age. I was probably only five or six, but I remember. I don't think Mom and Dad knew about it. It was just between Josh and me. It made me feel good to remember something that was just between Josh and me.

It made me feel awful too.

One of the grade nine boys asked me to dance. It's weird dancing with someone you've only seen in the hallways, or followed with Twyla and Jade. It's a good thing the music was loud.

Ryland wasn't there, which maybe was just as well

because after the baseball game, I'm even worse at talking to him. If he's around I'm always tripping or falling over something or stumbling through some joke that isn't even funny. Don't ask me why. If I ever figure out why I'm such a mess I'll do something about it. Anyway the truth is I probably had a good time because he wasn't there. Except I told Twyla otherwise.

Twyla decided it was a lousy dance, so she hauled me off to the washroom. Pretty soon I was saying that I was having a lousy time too. I thought it would make her feel better. Maybe it did make her feel better, but it made me feel worse. She went back out and blabbed all over that I thought it was a dumb dance. Now Travis and Jason probably think I don't even like them, and the grade nine girls who organized the dance must think I'm a stuck-up city kid.

But that's not what really bothers me. What really bothers me is that it reminded me of another time.

Remember the day at the hockey rink when John Keily was following you around? You dragged me out of earshot and made a face and asked me if I liked him.

"John Keily!" I said, and I can even remember making my face look like yours. "Naw, I don't really like him."

Well, I've got news for you. I lied. I was trying to say what I thought you wanted to hear. The truth is, I liked John Keily just fine. He was on one of the hockey teams that Josh helped coach and Josh liked him too, said he was a good player because he didn't just fly off the handle when the game got rough, he thought things through. And now that I've had time to think about it, I know that you already liked John. You just weren't sure how I would feel about it.

And what's more I know he liked you too. A lot.

So there.

The truth.

I'm sorry I wasn't smart enough to say it when you asked me.

That's who I thought about the rest of the way into the city, John Keily. I went into this crazy kind of daydream in which I met him in the mall and we went off somewhere and talked about things. About you. About everything.

Mom and I didn't go anywhere near our old school or the mall. We shopped at the far end of the city and Mom didn't even phone Aunt Stella, which will really make her mad if she finds out.

We shopped for groceries and winter clothes and Mom snuck off to buy some other things she didn't want me to know about.

On Monday I'm going to tell Jason and Travis I really did have a good time dancing with them. If I tell them straight, I hope they'll believe me.

I won't tell Twyla anything. I'll pretend the dance didn't even happen.

I'm good at that.

I've had a bit of practice.

30

Even without what was written in his report card, he knows his IA project is going well. He's started to sand the body of the plane, the wood is growing smooth, the angles softening. It's a biplane and both wings and the struts are cut out now. Soon they'll be ready to assemble. Except that Chalmers keeps hassling him.

"Maybe you could put a little gun turret there. Eh?"

He manages to drill the hole for the dowel that will join the engine block, nose cone, and propeller without the wood splitting or the hole going crooked. He's pleased even if he can't find the dowel because Chalmers has ditched it somewhere.

The class after woodworking is French. Hélène is standing in the hall with a sign.

"I've had it," she says. "Even my parents won't stand up for me. They tell me the same thing as everyone else, take the easy marks and be happy. It's stupid. I'm standing up for myself."

She's on strike until they change the rules about everyone having to take French even when you already speak it better than the teacher.

Sam surprises himself. He joins her. He writes *NON* across a double spread of his notebook. Below it, Hélène tells him what to write. Even then she has to correct the spelling.

A couple of girls from the class join them. And the kid, John, who's always watching from the back of the room comes up and talks to Hélène in the hall. They're talking quietly, but Sam can hear they're both talking French and a few minutes later the John kid is also making a sign. Sam looks at Hélène for explanation.

"He lived in Québec a couple of years ago. He likes the easy marks but he's going to support me anyway."

The French teacher takes one look, heads to the office and comes back with the principal.

"*En français*," says John quietly to Hélène. "*Et ne perds pas ton calme.*"

Hélène's French is fast and expressive. No one is scowling, so Sam's guessing she's managing to make her point without losing her cool. The French teacher replies to her in French. The principal mostly listens and when she does speak, her French is slower and sounds like the English-speaking politicians who struggle through French when the TV cameras are running. It doesn't take long before they come to an agreement. Hélène follows the principal down the hall. The teacher waves the rest of them toward the classroom.

"We've been trying to get the policy changed for years," she explains as they go through the door. "We just needed someone to make a formal complaint to make it happen."

He, John and the girls look at each other and shake their heads. They've known for a long time that adults are crazy.

31

Dear Amy,

Snow!

Even before I woke, part of me knew something was different. There's a special silence when it snows.

And there's lots of it. The hills are completely covered, huge and white against a sky that changed at noon from low and grey to high and clear and brilliantly blue. The bushes are bent into snow-gnomes. The trees are thick-limbed snow creatures from some icy planet. Snow-snakes run along the top of the corral fences.

After I finished chores with Dad, I went down to the spring. I had to see what it would be like with all the snow. I wasn't sure about riding Nelson on the steep, wet trails, so I just walked down with Sherbrooke.

Sherbrooke's a dog. Aunt Stella brought him out to the farm. She rescued him from a neighbour's backyard where he was always tied up, and the day she brought him out was one of those times when I liked Aunt Stella best of all. That day I didn't even mind her shoulder pads.

He moved right into the old doghouse beside the back steps. We don't tie him up. The first couple of days he didn't know exactly what to do with himself. It was kind of like "it's weird being free, but they feed me so maybe things will be OK." Now he just kind of acts like a dog. He sniffs around the yard. He barks at the magpies when they tease him. He follows Dad back and forth to the barn when he does the chores.

Dad doesn't want him to start chasing the horses, so he's taught him to stay outside the corrals. Sherbrooke thinks horses are pretty interesting, kind of like wild game. He lies on the ground and looks under the fence at them like he's a lion getting ready to pounce. The first couple of times he began inching forward Dad growled at him, so now he just lies there and watches. I think he's getting used to horses.

He followed on my heels all the way down to the spring, except for bounding off into the drifts out of sheer excitement when he couldn't help himself.

It was wonderful down there. The smell of the woods was strong and fresh as if the cold air had captured it and made it clearer somehow. Snow lay in the topmost tree branches like a canopy of lace overhead. It was piled high, high all around the sides of the troughs, and ice particles swirled and rustled in the corners with the moving water.

Some of the winter horses came down to drink while I was there. The change of weather had made them frisky and they clumped and slid down through the trees snorting and tossing their heads. They sniffed at the snow around the trough and they sniffed at the steam rising from the water and then they ran their noses across the surface, sucking the water in like vacuum cleaners.

Dad and Mom were shoveling a path between the garage and the house when I came up from the spring. They stopped and stood side by side to watch me as I waded through the snow on the far side of the yard. It felt good to see them standing like that, side by side. I think they were feeling pretty good too. That's the way new snow and blue sky make you feel. When I reached them, I stood there too.

Our house is at the base of the big hill, but it's also on top of its own smaller rise. Below are the show ring and the creek and a small valley that curls off into the distance like a little poem among the trees. It was all very, very beautiful.

"Just like a Christmas card," said Dad.

A Christmas card. If he'd used something else to describe it, things might have been OK. Instead, I could almost hear the hope fall out of the day, a dull, hissing sound in the snow.

"Josh loved Christmas," whispered Mom. "He would have loved the first snow."

They turned back to shoveling, Mom working toward the house, Dad toward the garage, me and Sherbrooke standing there not quite sure what to do next.

Just when, for a moment, something in the day had felt a little like hope.

I've been trying not to think about Christmas. It's hard. There are ads all over TV. At school, we've already begun practicing for the Christmas concert.

I think the concert is a big deal around here. It's not just the school kids that are in it, but everybody—like in stories about the pioneers where everyone and his dog is in the Christmas concert.

Grades seven, eight, and nine are the choir. Ms. Helpful is the conductor. She stands on the gym floor below the stage like a giant bird all painted in matching colours. She throws her wings around to tell us when to start and stop. She makes exaggerated movements with her beak to show us how to sing clearly, very round Os, and Ts that snap so hard her head jerks back. She's trying to get us to do the same, as if anyone would be caught dead looking like that.

Do you remember when you and I sang at the Christmas concert in grade five? That song about rheumatism and reindeer? We used talcum powder to turn our hair grey and you loaned me your old glasses so we'd both have a pair to pull down on our noses to look like real grannies. The teacher found the song, but it was your idea that we should dress up and act it out. I just went along with it the way I always did, because you had the best ideas. We hammed it up good. I heard someone say after that we two were the best… you and I.

And we were the best, together.

Oh Amy, I try and I try, but I can't get any of it to make sense.

I hate Christmas.

I don't know if we're going to have a tree. Dad and Mom don't talk about it. I'm scared to ask. I'm not even sure what I want the answer to be.

32

"Is that really me?" asks Cleo.

She needs a baby picture of herself for a project at school. There are two photo albums in the top of the closet. Sam knows which one to get down. He finds the photograph he's looking for, baby Cleo on her first day home from the hospital, a tiny bundle with a scrunched up face and a pink bow in the few wisps of hair on top of her head.

"I like the bow," she laughs.

Cleo is fascinated by the pictures that follow, the way the little bundle soon grows into a younger version of herself, big eyes and curly hair and little girl dresses. They haven't had the photo album down in a long time.

"Look at you, Sam!"

He has a thin neck, large ears, big grin. He's always doing something—balancing upside down on the sofa, making faces, wearing his pyjamas on his head. There are other people in the photos, but they're blurred, indistinct. A quick profile. A flash of glasses. There's one with an older lady he thinks is their grandmother, but Sam is busy making Cleo's curls go boing and Cleo's turning around to laugh at him, so that her face blocks everything except an elderly chin.

The photo record stops about the time Cleo is three. After that there are only school photographs, still in their plastic packages, slid between blank pages.

"Why don't we take pictures any more Sam?" asks Cleo.

Once again it comes like a wave rolling over him. Everett yelling at his mother.

"No photos! They'll see! Don't you know? They'll see!"

It was Sam's job, as always, to hide the offending object, quickly, before things could get worse. The box at the back of his closet, that's where he put the camera. It's probably there still. It wasn't the first thing he had to hide, or the last, or the worst. The worst thing he had to hide was a gun.

As soon as he feels the memory surfacing he pushes it away. He's not going there now.

"Look Cleo," he says, flipping back to the earlier pages of the book. "Do you remember the name of the rocking horse you used to ride?"

Cleo smiles. "Star," she says.

33

Dear Amy,

Something's happening, but I'm not sure what it is. So I just keep writing. If I can just feel you're there, it makes it easier. I hope you're not angry with me. Sometimes the things I tell you don't even sound important. A lot of the time I don't even know what I'm going to write until it all comes spilling out.

The night before last, Dad got tired of watching me sit in front of the TV and decided I could help him with the evening chores. So now after supper I put on my old clothes and trudge behind Dad out to the barn with Sherbrooke nudging and bunting at my mittened hand, begging me to throw snowballs for him to chase.

Even though it's getting really cold outside, it's still just the Arabs that are kept in the barn. The other horses are out on the land and I feel sorry for them sometimes, but Dad says they're tougher and used to it and will make out just fine.

Nelson is out with them. I visit him sometimes, just to make sure he's OK. I run my hands through his coat, as thick as rabbit's fur but coarser, heavier, and I scratch him behind his ears. Every day Dad walks down to the spring and breaks open any ice that's started to form on the water troughs. After Christmas he'll start putting out hay for them as well.

But the barn is where the Arabs are kept and coddled, fed their oats, and watered and brushed.

On weekends, when I do chores with Dad, we don't go out until the sun is up, but in the evening it's already been dark for an hour or more. Inside the barn the lights glow softly against the wood and it's warm and cold all at the same time. It almost feels like Christmas in the barns at night. The horses themselves are beautiful, their necks arch over the stall doors, their bright eyes and delicately pricked ears follow every movement and sound.

Sand Dancer gets some extra vitamins in her feed every night, because she's pregnant. And every night Dad tells me the same thing.

"If you're here alone when that mare starts foaling, and if it looks like she's having trouble, call the vet. Don't call the neighbours. They're all cattle farmers around here and if one of them decides you can pull an Arab colt the way they pull their calves, we'll have a dead mare and foal both."

I guess they really do pull calves when they need to. The whole idea scares me. How am I to know if Sand Dancer's having trouble? I didn't know how to ask Dad and I don't think it's covered in Twyla's sex book, no matter how interesting it is.

I don't know why Dad tells me every night. Sand Dancer's foal won't be born until spring, and anyway, it's not like he and Mom take off together any more.

Other than the chores morning and night, Dad hasn't much to do now that the snow is here. We don't have an indoor arena for working the horses, and it's too slippery on the show ring below the house.

A couple of times I've come home from school and

found him playing cards with Ellie's dad, Mr. Hanks, in our kitchen. I like Mr. Hanks. Sometimes, when I'm waiting for Ellie over at their place, he comes out and talks with me. He's quiet, like Ellie, but with big strong hands and thick arms and tiny blue eyes that look at you like they're interested in what you're saying. I think he likes to talk to kids. Actually, I think he likes to talk to anybody. Dad and he met at one of the fall farm sales and now he shows up once or twice a week and they play cards. Mr. Hanks is one of the cattle neighbours, but I know he's trying to learn about horses too, because I hear him asking Dad questions.

The rest of the time, Dad's off somewhere in the truck. I don't know where he goes. There aren't a lot of places around here unless he drives to Winosa, or maybe even all the way to the city. When he comes home at night he sits with a book in his hand, except he doesn't turn the page for hours on end.

And then we do chores.

"If that mare decides to foal when you're here alone…" he tells me.

34

It's Friday night and there's a movie on TV, computer animation that they both want to watch. He and Cleo are making popcorn in the kitchen with the air popper. It's one of the little things they like best, the large metal bowl filled almost to overflowing.

As the last pieces swirl out of the machine, he flips the switch to Off. A single, buried seed explodes from within the bowl and sends kernels flying across the counter. Cleo laughs and begins to gather them up.

He's been waiting for this kind of moment. There's something he wants to tell his little sister, but he's been waiting for a good time. Outside it's getting cold and dark, but inside the kitchen things feel safe and there's still the movie to look forward to.

"Cleo," he says, "if I ever do anything that scares you, you need to tell Mom, OK?"

She nods.

"I mean it Cleo," he says. "Even if it doesn't scare you very much, but it seems strange and it bothers you, I want you to tell her."

She looks at him and frowns.

"I heard you the first time, Sam. Don't keep saying it," she tells him.

Her attention returns to the bowl. She smiles at the drifts of warm, white kernels and asks,

"Do we put the butter on now?"

He wonders if she understands at all.

35

Dear Amy,

I have to tell you about the Christmas Concert. Some of it was like every other Christmas Concert in the world. Some of it wasn't. You would have liked the "wasn't" parts best.

The gym was packed with all kinds of people I'd never seen before. The little kids did the nativity scene and the little bit older kids did Santa and the Elves and we sang not too bad. In between all sorts of strange things happened.

There was a real live cow dressed as a reindeer. The same farmer brings her in every year. He leads the cow up there on stage and she and the farmer discuss all the political happenings for the last year. The farmer does all the talking and the cow, well she acts like a cow. You get the picture.

There was a super barbershop quartet, three short round guys and a tall skinny guy with a mustache who turned out to be Ms. Helpful. Ms. Helpful! It was the first time I'd seen her without lipstick. And she can actually sing!

The ladies' church group did a take-off of Batman. It was hilarious.

And the principal of the school, who is about six feet five inches tall and has a great, black mustache, came on stage in a nightshirt and bunny slippers and recited *T'was the Night Before Christmas*. He was great. That was just before Santa Claus came.

Our bus driver, Mrs. Gilbert, was Santa Claus. I'm not kidding. She fooled everybody too, most of the adults and the older kids and all the little kids of course, including her own little boy. The only reason I guessed is because I thought I saw something familiar about Santa's eyes and while I was staring and staring at them, the eyes looked up and Santa or the bus driver, or maybe both, winked at me.

After that I didn't want to give anything away, so I headed back to the classroom to get my coat and books. Ryland caught up with me in the hall.

"Did you guess who Santa is?" he asked.

I was feeling pretty good about having figured it out. I nodded. We were both kind of dressed up. The blue shirt he was wearing had neatened him up a little and made his eyes even bluer, but the same bit of hair was still flopping down over one eye and his pants were still hanging loose and crumpled around his hips. It was still Ryland. And, as always, he was watching for something, something interesting.

"Mr. Bremmer makes a good Santa doesn't he?" said Ryland.

Mr. Bremmer is the janitor. He's about the right size for Santa Claus, so Ryland might have made a mistake. Or he might not have. I kept trying to see what was going on in his eyes, but I couldn't be sure.

"If you think it's Mr. Bremmer," I said, "that's probably who it is."

Ryland's eyes laughed and I understood then. He didn't know. He'd seen Santa wink at me and was trying to get me to tell. I wasn't falling for it.

The classroom was noisy with Norm being a complete idiot, running around driving everyone crazy with mistletoe and Jason stealing it and ducking into the closet with

Ellie (they've liked each other ever since the dance) and Norm stealing it back and holding it over Travis's head and Travis telling Norm to smarten up or he'd thump him and Jade chasing Norm around the room with a plastic snake and Travis stealing the snake back and the mistletoe and chasing everyone else and Carolyn trying to get everyone to smarten up before Ms. Helpful came down to bawl us out.

I should have left then. Mom and Dad hadn't come to the concert, but it was late so I knew one of them would already be waiting outside in the car for me. I should have left, but I didn't.

Ryland was sitting on a desk watching the kids fooling around. I sat beside him. We talked for a while. It was easier to talk because any time there was an awkward moment, I could say something like "Do you want to know who Santa is?" which really got to him since he likes to know everything. Of course I never did tell.

It was hard to go home.

The house is decorated, but it still doesn't feel right. There's a big Christmas tree in the living room, Mom says Josh always loved big Christmas trees. I don't remember. It hurts too much to even try to remember. Mom's brought out all the little knick-knacks, magical and secretive, she's collected over the years and carefully set them around the house. Everywhere you look, you see something for Christmas, and on the piano she's set a picture of Josh she must have had enlarged while we were in the city. There's holly around it and a little angel tucked beside the corner.

Mom and I did the decorating last Saturday when Dad was away in the truck. When he came back, he took one look at it and went out to the barn. He didn't come back in for hours and hours and when he did he went straight to bed without saying a word to anyone.

Mom fell apart. She just sat at the table smoking cigarettes. Something else she bought in the city, I guess, except she used to smoke a long time ago. Maybe that's what she does in the basement. Maybe she doesn't throw clay around at all, just goes down and smokes cigarettes.

I wanted to ask her. I wanted to ask her a lot of things, including if there was something I could do that would help.

"I only wanted it to be nice for Josh," she kept saying. "I only wanted it to be nice for Josh."

It scared me Amy.

I haven't even been able to write about it until now, until the Christmas concert came along and for a moment things seemed real, because all week the silence in our house has been so loud it's like living completely and utterly alone.

36

"Hurry to Hardware Haven because even Santa loves to build!"

He's flipping channels on the TV after Cleo is in bed. Christmas ads play endlessly across the screen. At this time of night they're for power tools, jewellery, and computers. Most of them try to be funny, but he's not smiling.

He stops at a gathering of talking heads. It's not the kind of thing he usually watches, but oddly enough their words catch his interest. They're people who have lived in a war zone talking about what they feel like, even years and years afterwards.

"The way you are for a long time afterward is numb," the first head says.

"You've been shut down so long you can't feel any more," says the second head, nodding agreement. "You know you should be feeling things—about the past and about what's happening here and now, too—but you don't."

The third head does not nod or even join the conversation, not in a real way. The third head is talking to itself.

"It's like your soul is frozen."

There's something in what they are saying that Sam understands. How could that be? He's never lived in a country that was at war, never even left his own city. He's always lived with his family.

But he doesn't change the channel.

"What do you do?" asks a voice off screen.

"You let yourself remember little by little," the first head answers.

"You find someone to help you, if you can," says the second.

"You keep going," says the third.

37

Dear Amy,

This morning Ellie's dad came over. Mom had already snuck off downstairs and Dad had just come in from doing chores. I didn't go with him. I haven't been out in the barn all week. These days Dad doesn't want to be around anyone. It's a feeling that hangs around him like ice.

When Mr. Hanks turned up at the door, however, I didn't know what to do so I let him in.

Dad was OK at first, he and Mr. Hanks even started a game of cards on the table, but it didn't last long. After just a couple of hands, Mr. Hanks said something about Christmas and that was it. Dad said he had work to do in the barn, put on his coat, and walked out.

I didn't see it happen, I was in the living room watching TV, but I heard it. I expected Mr. Hanks to leave too, but he didn't. He came and sat in the living room with me and watched cartoons, which was the only thing I could get on the TV because we don't have a dish and there's no cable out here. Watching cartoons with Mr. Hanks felt pretty weird.

An ad came on and Mr. Hanks picked up the TV controller and turned the sound down. Things were still happening on the screen, but without any sound they seemed to be happening three worlds away and the TV screen seemed smaller.

Mr. Hanks cleared his throat and leaned forward with his elbows on his knees and looked at his hands. He looked at me and then he looked back at his hands.

He leaned back, and I knew he'd decided something because he almost relaxed, almost but not quite. The cartoons had come on again, but neither of us turned up the sound.

"What's wrong around here, Kate?" he asked. "I don't just mean today. Ever since you moved here something's been wrong. What is it?"

From the top of the piano, Josh's picture looked across at us. Josh's picture draped in holly and tinsel. How could I keep from looking at it?

Mr. Hanks followed my eyes to the picture. He crossed the room and stood in front of it. He looked at me and then back at the picture again. We have the same eyes, Josh and I, the same chin, the same smile. Brother and sister, once upon a time.

"When did it happen?" he asked at last.

"Last February," I said. "February 15th."

"A car crash?" he asked.

"No," I said.

I've never had to tell before, Amy. I felt cold all over. I wasn't even sure I could say the words.

"He had a gun. Not my brother, some guy on the street out front. He was crazy, shouting and screaming, and then he began shooting, shooting at the store just because it was there. There wasn't even any reason and he didn't care. He didn't care how many people were inside. Or who they were. Or whether they were working there or drinking coffee or walking by or buying candies for their friend. At a Quick Mart store."

I didn't tell him the rest of it. I didn't tell him that the guy killed himself too. Why didn't he just do that in the first place and leave everyone else alone? Why Amy?

The look on Mr. Hanks face is exactly why Mom and Dad didn't want me to tell anyone about it. It's like laying sorrow on sorrow. When you tell someone, it's like—for a minute—one of their own kids dies. But only for a moment. Because then they realize it isn't their child, their child is still OK, and even though they don't want you to see it, the tiniest shade of relief sneaks in. Relief because it wasn't their child. But your brother, or son, or best friend, is still dead.

Mr. Hanks was better than most. He didn't try to say things when he didn't know what to say. I think he was pretty shaken because for a long time he didn't say anything at all.

"No wonder," he said at last. "No wonder."

"Mom and Dad don't want people around here to know. They just want to get on with things."

Mr. Hanks turned to look at me.

"They aren't doing a very good job of it, are they?" he asked.

"No," I whispered.

And then he was gone.

38

A week before Christmas his mom comes home with a small tree. He's relieved. It looks like they're doing Christmas after all.

"For Cleo's sake," she tells him. "She's just a little girl. Little girls deserve Christmas."

He's been saving his bus ticket money. He's got presents for both of them, Cleo and his mom too.

They decorate the apartment, all three of them working together to empty the box from the hall closet of its lights and balls, silver streamers and Christmas characters.

"What happened to Rudolph's ear?" asks Cleo, holding up a friendly looking—but lopsided—creature.

"Frostbite," he answers without blinking an eye. "The year they had the big storm at the North Pole. It doesn't hurt. He's kind of proud of it. It's kind of a badge of honour."

He doesn't look at his mother. Prefers his own story to the one she will know, the one where they came out to open their stockings and found all eight reindeer nailed to the mantelpiece. Rudolph was the only one he could save and only because Everett didn't notice.

How old was he that year? Maybe the same age as Cleo. Maybe younger.

Christmas morning there are stockings for him and Cleo both, even though he knows he's too old for a stocking. There are games and clothes and toys, at least one thing they asked for and all kind of things they wouldn't have thought of asking for, which is what you get from hampers, but he's still glad.

His mom sings carols as she cooks the turkey. Her friend arrives with a new boyfriend and a bottle of wine and two kinds of casseroles. The boyfriend is the nice kind. It feels like Christmas. A real Christmas. It makes Sam nervous. He keeps expecting the door to open and Everett to come in and things to change. Some kind of fight to start. Or someone knocking the tree down. He's happy and he feels guilty.

He looks up to see his mother holding the phone out to him.

"It's for you, Sam," she says. "we're pretty noisy out here. Maybe you'd like to take it in the bedroom."

He thinks maybe it's Chalmers, phoning to gloat about whatever someone stole for him, or maybe his grandmother, who lives on the other side of the country in a place where they have to care for her all the time but she still sometimes remembers to phone. But it's not.

"Sammy! That you son?"

He swallows hard.

"Hey, Dad. Merry Christmas."

"How you doing? Are you surprised to hear from your old dad? I meant to get some presents in the mail to you, but it just got too busy here so I thought I'd better at least phone so you know I didn't forget you entirely. I bet you got lots of presents anyway. Did you?"

"Got lots of presents, Dad."

"Good. That's good. What about your sister. She get presents too?"

"Cleo's fine, Dad," he says. "She's got lots of presents."

"Cleo. That's right. And how's your mom. You taking care of her? That was bad about Everett. I called then, but nobody was answering I guess."

"We're OK, Dad."

"Good, good. Well I better go, son. I'm using a friend's phone. These things cost a bit."

"I got a real good report card, Dad. And Cleo's in grade two. You should see how big she is."

"That's good, son," he says. "You'll both put me to shame. That's what you'll do. I'll stop by next time I'm West. You'll open your door and there will be your old dad. That'd be good eh?"

"That'd be great, Dad," he says.

But the line is already dead.

Later, when Cleo is in bed and the others have left, his mother and he sit side by side on the couch.

"Was he doing okay? Your Dad?" she asks.

"He was with friends. He sounded okay," says Sam.

"Did he ask about me?" she says.

"I told him you were doing good, real good," says Sam.

His mom looks out the window at the lights along the street. When she talks again, her voice has a tone he doesn't hear very often.

"It wasn't Everett that drove your dad away, you know that Sam. We hadn't been getting along for a long time, your dad and I. Everett was just the last straw. It's different when it's not your own flesh and blood. And you know how Everett was."

Sam wants her to stop but he knows she can't.

"I couldn't throw him out," said his mom. "You can't throw your own son out. Not when no one else will help him. Not the school. Not the social services. Not the police. He ended up leaving anyway, but he always knew he could come home if he had to. It was all I could give him, a place to come to if he had to. I'd do the same for you. I'd do the same for Cleo."

His only Christmas wish in the whole world is that she will never have to.

39

Dear Amy,

It's the time of year when winter never ends. Every day is cold and dark and frozen and that's how I feel too, most of the time. Sometimes in the morning, standing waiting for the bus, I feel so alone I can hardly stand it.

Dad is gone. Christmas and New Years came and went and it was bad. When it was over I came home from school on the third day of classes and Dad was gone. I'm madder than I can tell you at him for running out. I'm mad at Mom too. For hiding in the basement. For letting him go.

Mom didn't fall apart the way I thought she would. Instead, she started planning. It was almost as if she'd been waiting for something like this to happen. I think I've figured out something about Mom. She's good in a crises, it's the long parts in between that she has trouble with.

She had everything planned by the time I got home from school. It was only three days ago. It seems like years.

Mr. Limster would come down and stay at the farm himself. We'd pack our bags and move in with Aunt Stella. Mom would look for a job.

She went on and on about how she'd been wrong. She'd been wrong to bring us out to the country and cut us off from everything. She'd been wrong, and she was going to make it right.

I didn't want to listen to her plans. I couldn't. I couldn't even think properly. I just wanted to get away from her. I wanted to get out of the house and away from her. The Arabs were in the barn and someone had to do the evening chores. I changed into my barn clothes and headed out the door.

I remember the way the wind felt when I stepped out the door, cold and biting and uncaring. A few thin snowflakes were dropping from the winter sky. As I walked in my big boots across the yard, it felt like the whole world had come down upon me in the darkness.

I realized something I didn't want to know. Dad had been planning it. He'd taught me to do the evening chores because he'd been planning it all along so he could leave without even saying good-bye.

And then I began to feel awful, really awful in a way I'd never felt before. If I hadn't gone out to the barn those first few mornings, if I hadn't shown him I could learn to do the chores in the first place, if I'd just left everyone alone the way they wanted to be, maybe he'd still have been here. I was so angry I couldn't even cry. I couldn't do anything except be angry. I barely even noticed Sherbrooke running in circles, rolling in the snow, and tossing something over his back into the air.

Finally he stuffed something right into my mittened hand and bunted it so hard with his nose I couldn't ignore him. I lifted my hand. A stick. A Sherbrooke stick. The thing he loved best since he'd come to the country was chasing sticks. I held it so tightly I thought it would snap. I can feel it in my hand still.

I turned around in the middle of the yard and walked back into the house. I told Mom I wasn't leaving.

I can't believe I said it, but I did. You would have been proud of me.

Mom thought I was crazy at first. But I didn't cry. And I didn't yell. And I didn't even mention Sherbrooke. I just told her I wasn't leaving. I didn't want to leave. I wasn't going to leave unless it was the only, only way.

Mom looked at me a long time. It felt like she was seeing me from way, far away. Way far away. And then something shifted and we were in the same room together, close to each other, and I felt like for the first time in a long, long while she was really looking at me.

"I thought you didn't like it here," she said. "All summer you went on and on about how awful it was. How bored you were. How there were no people. How you didn't want to be here."

Had I really done that? Had I really complained so loudly?

"That was in the summer," I said.

After a little bit, Mom got her coat and boots and we both went out to the barn to do the chores. It's not hard, really. It takes time, but it's not hard and it's not like Mom's afraid of horses. She doesn't ride, but she's lived on a farm with animals before.

When we came back inside, Mom said we'd try it for a week, she and I. She phoned Mr. Limster to let him know what was going on. She didn't phone Aunt Stella.

So for now, Mom and I are staying alone.

I have to stay Amy. This is a good place for keeping secrets. I'm not sure I could keep writing to you from anywhere else.

And I'm not ready to go it alone.

40

There's something about Chalmers that has changed since Christmas. There's an added edginess about him. An extra streak of mean. Maybe he's just been cooped up inside too long because of winter. Maybe it's something more. Sam's seen him hanging out near the place where he "shops," even in the cold weather, same corner where the guy with the tattoo hangs out.

Whatever it is, he's started to play Sam again.

In IA a wood rasp goes missing.

"Sam, didn't you have it last?" calls Chalmers from the back of the room.

Another day, one of the sanding machines is jammed.

"You were just on this, Sam. Did you screw it up again?" calls Chalmers.

Sam's biplane is in the last stages, but he knows for sure now that it's not going to get done. Chalmers isn't going to let him finish.

He has to stay at the back of the room, away from the machines, away from Chalmers and his little gang. He can't let Chalmers get to him, can't let him pin anything on him. The term will be over in a few weeks. If he can stay out of range until then, he'll be OK.

Maybe.

41

Dear Amy,

Here I am deciding I want to stay, and all of a sudden school is getting weird.

Ms. Helpful decided to give us a talk yesterday about girls and boys. Actually she just talked to the girls. The French teacher talked to the boys. I'd have rather been in on the boys' session.

Schools every place else in the universe have co-ed sex education. We have a girls-only talk by Ms. Helpful and she'd didn't really say anything except we should look out for ourselves and if we have any questions we should come and see her.

I don't care. Late night TV's got lots of sex information one way or another, even without the cable channels. And I may not have Internet but some of the magazines my mom gets have all kinds of articles about sex that don't pretend it's something people aren't interested in the way Ms. Helpful did. I had to get out the book Twyla gave me and actually look up some of the words they used in the last magazine issue Mom got.

I like Twyla's book. It's a bunch of definitions so you can look things up, but you can also read your way through it and discover all kinds of good stuff. I sandwich it between the pages of my science book just in case Mom walks in. I'm pretty sure she wouldn't mind, but I just kind of like to read it on my own. I was right. It doesn't talk about how you know if a mare's having trouble foaling. But I know about some things now that Twyla and the other kids only think they know about, even though they've had more firsthand experience. In fact I think Twyla better take her book back and study it really hard, especially if she keeps chasing after Aaron the way she is.

Gord is the guy she used to like, but now she likes Aaron. He fooled around a lot last year, so his parents tried sending him to a private school. I guess it didn't work, because now he's back here.

A lot of the grade nine girls like him. I don't know if that's got something to do with what's going on or not.

Tuesdays and Thursdays, when the Phys-Ed teacher is at another school, the big gym stays closed all day. Twyla and some of the other girls and a bunch of the grade nine boys including Aaron sneak into it at lunchtime. Sometimes Twyla takes Jade and me with her. All the lights are out and it feels huge in the dark and everyone runs around like you do when you play hide and go seek, except that's not what it is, and you have to do it really quietly so none of the teachers know we're there. It's weird too because there's something exciting about it that I haven't explained very well. I haven't quite figured out what's going on.

I don't care anyway. Doing the chores with just Mom and I is harder than I thought, especially cleaning out the stalls. I just want to get through this week.

42

It's cold but he doesn't mind the cold. His mom's friend has found him a jacket that looks great and is almost new. He's strong from striding down the hill after school. He's gotten so fast that as long as he gets out of class in decent time, he can walk home even on regular days and still be home to take care of Cleo when his mom leaves for work.

The kid who lives near the school has had him over a couple of times on Saturdays. The family likes him, doesn't ask questions any more. On most Sundays he ends up at the library playing video games. When he's out of the apartment there's more room for Cleo to have friends over. He remembers what it was like to have friends over, remembers why he stopped. But seeing Cleo makes him happy.

The other reason he goes out is because Chalmers keeps phoning the apartment.

"Hey, get over here. I'll beat the pants off you on the system." Or, "Hey, I'm headed out. Meet me at the corner."

Usually there's someone yelling in the background or maybe it's just the TV. In any case, Sam makes sure he always has an excuse ready.

And then a different type of call. Chalmers voice is slurred.

"Hey, you creep, you're not half the man your brother was. You know that, don't you? Just 'cause you made off with your brother's gun, that doesn't mean you're tough enough to use it."

Sam's confused. He doesn't have the gun from the Quick Mart. Why would Chalmers think he has it? Sam listens hard, tries to piece things together.

"You were a little twerp back then and you're still a little twerp," slurs Chalmers. "Scared little twerp ditching a gun on your big, bad brother. Bet you haven't even had the guts to go back and pick it up. I'm right aren't I. It's still there, isn't it."

Chalmers isn't talking about the Quick Mart, Sam realizes. He's talking about the apartment, years ago. The first time Everett got his hands on a gun, the first time Sam knows about at least.

That day comes rushing back with the hot breath of panic. The coldness of metal. The sound of Everett yelling. And Sam himself racing frantically out of the apartment, into the hall and down the stairs.

Nine years old and he knew he had to get the gun out of reach of Everett, hide it, hide it.

It seems impossible to Sam. Don't think about it, he tells himself. Don't think about it. The gun is gone. Hidden.

OK, Chalmers might have lived in the apartment building back then, might have heard the yelling, might have known what it was about. But he can't possibly know where it is. He's bluffing. Guessing. Trying to push Sam into making a mistake.

Sam hangs up the phone.

With luck, when Chalmers sobers up, he won't even remember that he called.

43

Dear Amy,

We're still here. It's been almost two weeks now and Mom and I are doing OK. Morning and night we do chores together. It doesn't take us nearly as long as it did at first. In the middle of the day, Mom goes down and checks the water trough and counts the winter horses. She says she doesn't know if she'd recognize if anything was wrong with them or not, but at least she knows they're all there.

On the weekends I help her with the mid-day check, too, and we've begun putting out hay in the field for the winter horses. We phoned Mr. Limster to find out how much.

Do you know something? I think Mom likes doing the outside work. I think she likes getting out in the barn early, early in the morning when the horses are only half awake and the sounds are loud and muffled all at once, the water splashing into the bucket, the clunk of hooves as the horses turn in their stalls. Sometimes she even tells me to stay in bed, she'll do them herself, and when she comes in there's something about her that's different. It's not peaceful, but it's quiet. Just for a few moments anyway.

A couple of times we've had to go down to the spring on days when the cold seems to suck the breath right out of your lungs. The horses watch for us, to see if we are going to stop where the hay is stacked behind the corral fence. Throwing bales over the corral fence is hard work and the sweat trickles down your back and makes you feel prickly as the hay itself, but I like to cut the twine and pull it free so the hay falls apart. The horses mill around and I always make sure Nelson gets a couple of handfuls of oats from a stash I keep deep in my pockets.

The Arabs we keep inside except for an hour or so in the warmest part of the day. Their stalls get mucked up pretty quickly and I've had lots of experience with a pitchfork lately.

But I miss Dad. I'm mad at him and I miss him all at once.

I don't think he expected us to stay here after he'd gone. He knew we could get by for a few days, but I don't think he expected us to really stay.

I wonder if he'd be surprised.

I wonder if he'd care.

44

The IA teacher is a few minutes late getting to class. Chalmers and his buddies are busy around the machines. They call Sam over to see what they're doing, but he doesn't get drawn in. When the teacher arrives and goes to demonstrate on the machine, sparks fly everywhere.

Chalmers guffaws loudly.

"Now you've really done it, Sam!" he calls out.

This time it's serious. The look on the teacher's face says all that and more. Sam knows he has to speak up.

"It wasn't me," Sam says. "Anyone will tell you. I wasn't near it."

"Yeah right," says one of Chalmers' followers.

"We all saw you," says another.

The teacher isn't clueless, he knows about Chalmers. But he doesn't know as much about his little circle of friends. The followers have never spoken up like this before.

"I wasn't anywhere near it," insists Sam.

He looks around the room for someone to back up his story. No one offers. They might not be in Chalmers' gang but they know how much trouble he can cause. And Chalmers has never let any of the others make friends with Sam.

Still, the teacher hesitates, tries to think things through. Who to believe? How best to handle this? It's just the moment Chalmers has been waiting for, all the attention in the world. He throws up his arms.

"You gonna believe me, or you gonna believe someone whose killer of a brother shot up the Quick Mart?"

Something bursts red in Sam's head. He wants to shout and yell, throw things, break things, punch Chalmers over and over and over.

But this is how strong the fear is. The fear holds his arms frozen to his sides. The fear that if he ever lets the anger out, the kind of madness that explodes, he'll be like Everett, and he'll never be able to stop it.

He turns and walks out the classroom door.

45

Dear Amy,

I found out what goes on in the gym. I was right. It isn't hide and go seek. It's hide and wait for whoever finds you and see what happens next. The boys chase the girls until they catch them and then if it's a girl they like they try to kiss her or if it's a girl they're just curious about, they feel under her shirt or anywhere else they can. Stupidest thing I ever heard of.

I have some questions I want to ask someone. How come in almost all the teen magazines the way you get together with a boy is he asks you on a date? Or maybe you even ask him. Anyway, someone asks someone else and they get a chance to say yes or no and then they get a chance to worry about things like what to wear and how much make-up to put on and maybe even how much your tongue is involved in French kissing. Then, if you like each other, you have another date and maybe you go a bit further. And somewhere down the line—but only after you've done other fun things too, like going to the beach or a movie or some really great club or something, which is totally impossible out here even if a person was old enough—somewhere down the line you get really hot for each other, but you've had a chance to read all the magazine articles about grappling in the dark and you can decide what to do.

How come life isn't like the magazines?

Lon Davis caught me in the gym. I don't even like Lon

Davis. I definitely didn't want him feeling me up. My shirt ripped when I pulled away from him.

I lied about the shirt. I said I caught it on a locker. I don't know whether I should have told on Lon Davis. I didn't, but I won't go in the gym any more. Twyla tried to talk me into going in with her yesterday.

"No," I said. "It's stupid."

The way she looked at me, I figured she was just going to take off without me. It made me feel awful, Amy. I didn't realize how much I liked Twyla until that moment. But I wasn't going back in the gym.

I didn't know what was going on in Twyla's mind. It's hard to tell with her. You'll think she's thinking one thing, and then she'll say something entirely different. That's what happened this time.

She looked at me a long time. Finally she shrugged.

"Come on," she said.

She wasn't headed to the gym, so I followed her. We went into the grade nine homeroom. She swiped a deck of cards from one of the desks. We sat at the back of the room and she taught me how to play a game called Bullshit. When Lon, Aaron, Gord, and some of the girls came looking for her to go to the gym, she answered for both of us.

"No," she said. "It's stupid."

So they went without her, all except Gord.

"Hey," he said. "You swiped Aaron's cards."

Twyla just shrugged and dealt him into the game.

Gord's a nice guy when you give him a chance.

And I guess Twyla's OK after all.

46

He stays home sick for three days, but he's not too sick to intercept the phone or take the messages off the answering machine while his mother's asleep. Saturday afternoon, however, Cleo answers the phone and gives it to their mom.

He sees the energy go out of her. She takes it into the other room to talk.

"It was the school," she says when she comes out. "About what happened in Woodworking. About you not going to class."

"I'll go back on Monday," he says. "You don't have to deal with it."

"I told them we'll come in together," she says.

She doesn't ask him to explain. He thinks he knows why. Everett wouldn't have told the truth. She doesn't want to test Sam. Doesn't want an answer that turns out to be a lie. What would she do then?

Maybe it's just as well. He doesn't know where he'd start.

Cleo plays quietly, quietly all weekend. Tiptoes around. Helps to clear the table. How quickly we learn our roles, he thinks.

47

Dear Amy,

Aunt Stella has found out about us. Mom's been trying to put her off the last couple of weeks, saying the winter roads were too dangerous, but yesterday she drove out unannounced from the city.

You should have heard her. She started talking about separation agreements and divorce papers. She told Mom we never should have moved. She told Mom if Dad was going to leave anyway it would have been a lot easier if he'd left us in the city where we used to live. She said he should be paying child support and relocation money and a thousand other things.

Mom told Stella she's worried about him.

It's the first time I've heard her say that. Before, she was just as mad at him as I was.

After Stella went, Mom took me down in the basement. She showed me what she'd been working on since last summer. I was right, she's been smoking cigarettes like crazy down there, there were butts everywhere. But she'd been building things too, hand building with coils of clay.

I don't know what they are but they're ugly, twisted and misshapen, thick, grotesque. Mom says the way they're made, thick and solid, they'd explode if she put them in a kiln. She said when she first realized what she'd done she thought she'd wasted all her work, but she's glad now that's the way they are. She can't ever fire them, can't ever make them permanent. Maybe one day they'll turn back to clay.

Then she said something strange to me.

"I don't come down here any more since your dad left," she said. "He has to carry his own sorrow now."

It's better without him here, Amy. No, that's not right. It's not better for me. I want him here. Even though I'm so mad at him I could cry, I want him here.

But it's better for Mom.

48

On Monday he walks Cleo to the corner by her school and then goes back to the apartment. They aren't due at the school until ten.

They ride the bus together but at least there aren't other kids around. He sits in the outer office while they talk to his mother first. Then they call him in. There are three others in the room, the IA teacher, the principal and a counsellor. The IA teacher is holding Sam's airplane, unfinished but with wings and struts in perfect balance, a propeller that spins freely. Only the wheels need to be attached.

"I don't see any way that a student who has taken the time to work so carefully on a project would do anything on purpose to the equipment," he says. "However we can't prove things either way. I'm giving you a passing grade, but it's been decided that you'll spend the last few periods in the detention room doing homework."

That's all there is. The IA teacher excuses himself from the room with the airplane still in his hands.

Of course it's not really over. The school knows now. He can feel it in the room with the two who are left. They're judging them both, his mother, himself. They're weighing them, turning them around and around, something strange they've never seen before. Sometime, maybe not today, but sometime soon, they'll say they want to help. They'll think they have some kind of understanding.

His mother's eyes touch his own for just a moment. They're both thinking exactly the same thing. The three people in front of them couldn't understand even the tiniest bit, not in a thousand, thousand years. He wonders that his mother can keep so calm, so quiet. Then he remembers how much practice she's had. How many offices, just like this one, she must have sat in.

He goes back to class, slips in with the others when periods change. They know. All of them know. He can tell from the stares, the whispers. Hélène says hi so quietly he can barely hear it.

He's lived with it once already but it's different this time. He didn't exactly have friends at the old school, you can't make friends when you can't even have someone to your house to watch TV, but at least they were used to him. They'd all gone to class together for a couple of years.

Here he's just started to know people, maybe make friends.

Whatever relief he felt after being in the office hardens around him into the shell he knows pretty well by now. At lunch he wanders off to sit on his own behind one of the pillars. The kid he's gotten to know, the one whose house he's visited, comes over.

"I heard about your brother. I guess if you're sitting over here it means it's true," he says.

Sam eats his sandwich. Waits for what's coming next.

"I remember reading in the paper he was nuts," says the kid. "Your brother, I mean. Was he?"

Those aren't the words the paper used. A history of mental disorder and violence, that's what it said. Words on a page. Meaningless. Sam has no intention of telling anyone anything about Everett. He looks at the kid steadily.

"I'm not nuts," he says.

"I didn't say you were," says the kid. "I was just asking about your brother."

Sam isn't cutting him any slack. He just waits. The kid turns to go back to the others. At the last minute he calls casually.

"See you in the gym."

It's a crumb, tossed over his shoulder. Sam knows he's not too proud to take it. He also knows not to kid himself about how much it actually means. They'll put up with him in house leagues, but it will be a long time before anyone asks him over.

If the kid tells his family, a long time will be never.

49

Dear Amy,

I've got to learn to keep my mouth shut.

Do you remember how last fall someone asked me if I liked Drew and I said yes because I do like him and the word went back and forth and pretty soon we were walking around holding hands? Well, I've got news for you. I never liked Drew that way. I just liked him as a kid, not a boyfriend or anything, but the next thing I knew everyone thought we were engaged and about to be married.

Well, I did it again.

We went to see a movie in the city last week. It was just our class and we all trooped on board Mrs. Gilbert's bus. It was great fun because we never get to ride the bus as a class, and we never get to go anywhere, let alone to a movie together. Everyone had a good time, and Ryland and I talked a bunch and threw popcorn back and forth. But just as we started getting back on the bus to go home, people started asking me things.

I tell you, even riding the bus is not like the magazines. In the magazines Ryland would have walked up and said "Kate, do you want to sit together?" But of course that's not what happened.

What happened is Travis asked me. I tried to ignore him, but Carolyn heard it and cornered me and pointed out how I always said how nice Travis was and how people shouldn't ignore other people and to make a long story short, I ended up sitting with Travis.

But Ryland sat in the seat behind me and there's a space between the bus seat and the window that's kind of squishy but you can slip your hand through. I held hands with Ryland all the way home.

Secretly.

I hope it was secretly. I didn't want to embarrass Travis. Travis is great. He'd be perfect for Carolyn.

From now on if anyone asks me if I like someone, I'm going to smile and look mysterious and pretend my lips are stuck together permanently with crazy glue.

50

Hélène has been speaking to him all along, but the last couple of days it's been in a weird kind of way. Finally she pulls him over, says she really has to talk to him. They sit behind the pillar in the lunchroom. It's where he sits anyway.

"There's something you need to know about John," she says. "John from our class."

Sam nods.

"He knew them," says Hélène.

"Knew who?" he asks.

"From the Quick Mart. Whoever it was your brother killed."

The words seem to knock the breath from his lungs. Of course that's what it is. Why didn't he see it coming? It had to happen. Someday. Someplace. It's a city, but even a city isn't that big.

"Did he tell you that?" asks Sam.

"I heard it from talk going around," says Hélène. "But I wanted to be sure before I said anything, so I asked him. He's known all along, recognized you on the first day of class. I guess there was a picture of you and your mom coming out of some building, a picture in the newspaper."

It wasn't just in the newspaper, it was on the TV news too. The real reason his mom changed to night shifts.

"Anything else?" asks Sam.

"He's not exactly the type to volunteer information," says Hélène. " Do you want me to ask him?"

Sam shakes his head. No. Hélène looks relieved.

"I thought you should know, but now that I've told you I feel like some kind of traitor, except I don't know whose side I've ratted on," she says.

Join the club, he thinks. Join the club.

When he gets back to class that afternoon, he's careful not to look at John any more or any less than before. What could he possibly say that would be of any real help?

Let it go for now, Sam thinks. Just let things go the way they are for now.

51

Dear Amy,

It's been a year since the Quick Mart. All week it was like trying to swim in a heavy, grey cement. Every time the phone rang or we heard a car approaching on the main road—not very often for either of them—I could see Mom jump. I guess we were thinking the same thing. Maybe it would be Dad. Except I was hoping it would be him and Mom, I think she was hoping it wouldn't be. She's worried about him, but I don't think she wants to face him yet.

I stayed home on the 15th. I didn't even ask Mom about it, I just did. Last spring we scattered Josh's ashes near a stream in the mountains where he and Dad liked to fish, so there wasn't a cemetery to visit and now the mountain roads are closed with snow. Maybe it was a mistake to take his ashes there.

But Aunt Stella showed up out of the blue in the morning. She said there was going to be a one-year memorial service for Josh at a church near the Quick Mart. The teams he coached and the Cub Pack he helped with all wanted to do something to remember him. They'd been trying to contact us but Mom hadn't told anyone where we were going when we moved. Even when they told Stella about it, she hadn't known whether or not to tell Mom which I guess is why she drove out, that and just to be with us.

Mom said over and over she wasn't going to the memorial, but at noon she suddenly changed her mind. She had Stella phone Mr. Hanks, just so he'd know we were gone for the day, and then she told me to ride with Stella, she'd follow in our own car so we could come home right after.

It was OK riding in with Stella. Neither of us said very much the whole trip, but we didn't have to. Stella doesn't always understand, but Stella loved Josh too.

With the winter roads it was after three by the time we got there, and the service had just ended. Maybe it wasn't the roads, maybe Mom planned it that way. Cars were driving away. Some kids were walking home. They didn't see me, but I recognized some of them from a distance. One of them was John Keily. I couldn't go up and talk to him, Amy. I'm sorry. I wanted to, but I couldn't. I don't know if you want to hear the rest of this.

There were flowers in the church, and candles and a picture of Josh with notes and troop badges and team crests around it. People do remember. They do. Even if there aren't a church and candles and flowers. They remember just as strongly. They care just as much.

I stayed at the back of the church. I guess I'm not as brave as I think I am. I couldn't go any further. Stella stayed with me.

Mom went right up to the altar and looked at the flowers and candles and the picture. It was while she was standing there that a lady slipped in quietly from a side door. I don't think she saw Mom because of the flowers and because they were both so silent. I don't think Mom saw her either, not at first. They just stood there side by side. And then something shifted slightly and they were looking at each other.

She wasn't one of the parents, Amy. No. That's not true.

She was a parent. She must have been waiting until she thought it was all over and everyone had left, just the way we had waited. She was his mom. The guy with the gun. The guy whose name I don't ever want to know.

Amy, it felt like the church was going to fall down. It felt like the wood and the windows and the steeple and the glass were all too heavy and it was just going to collapse. Even Stella felt it beside me. I heard her draw in her breath.

Mom's back grew very stiff, and she turned her head forward again. But I could see down the aisle, Amy. Mom and the lady's hand were side by side on the rail and just for a moment, a long, timeless moment, their hands shifted, one to the other, and each held tightly onto the other's hand.

Then the woman slipped away out the side door again.

We didn't stop for supper on the way home. Mom said there were chores to do, except when we got home everything had been done. Mr. Hanks was sitting in our yard in his pickup truck with a pan of cinnamon buns Ellie's mom had made.

Mom thanked him. He waved her into the house along with the cinnamon buns. He put a hand on my arm just as I was going to follow her.

"Don't give up hope, Kate," he said to me.

After supper, I went out to check things in the barn. Everything was fine. Cattle rancher or horse rancher, I guess they all know how to do chores. It was kind of funny though. A winding line of dark blue marks in the moonlit snow showed that where he'd come out of the barn, he'd strayed from the path to walk along the corral fence.

I followed his tracks, big and deep and wide apart, so

that I had to stretch to place my boot print within his, even if he is only about as tall as I am. I found where he'd stopped. It took me a few minutes to remember, but it was where there'd been a loose rail in the fence. I couldn't see very well because the yard light was behind me, but he must have spiked a couple of nails into it because it didn't feel loose any more. As I stretched my legs to follow the tracks back to the main path I knew I was really just delaying going inside.

I hate this day.

It's not over just because a year passes. It's never over.

52

He gets called to the office to see the counsellor the way he knew he would.

"How are you doing these days, Samuel?"

"I'm OK."

"You making friends?"

"Sure."

"Anyone hassling you?"

"Nope."

"We can talk about anything at all," she says. "Is there anything you'd like to talk about? "Does it run in families like a disease? Does everyone hate you forever? How much is your fault? Does your mom ever stop crying? How do you know if it's starting to happen to you, too?"

"I'm OK."

He doesn't tell the counsellor, of course, but what he's really worried about at the moment is Chalmers. The whole school knows now about Sam and Everett being brothers but the feeling that Chalmers still has power over Sam is stronger than ever.

They don't have classes together any more, but at school he goes out of his way to walk past Sam in the hall. He doesn't say anything, just smirks at Sam, gives him a knowing look. He's started to phone again, but he's not ragging on Sam. He jokes about their little misunderstanding. He tries to jolly Sam into meeting him. It's pretty clear he hasn't forgotten the gun, but the scary part about Chalmers is that he twists things around, including twisting himself around. You never know what direction he's coming from.

Sam's at his locker one day when he feels someone standing behind him, hears a click. He turns very, very slowly.

He doesn't realize how tense he is until he sees that it's only the IA teacher, fishing his keys out of his jacket pocket.

"I'm just going down to the shop so some of the older kids can work on the machines over the lunch hour," he says. "If you wanted to finish your plane, you could probably get the wheels on."

The teacher leaves without expecting an answer. Sam thinks of the little plane. He hasn't forgotten it, the way it balanced in his hands, the feel of the wood. Is this why the IA teacher held onto it? So he could give Sam a chance to finish even if he couldn't officially let him back into class?

Sam pretends to rearrange the books in his locker. He doesn't want anyone to think he's walking with a teacher. When at last he turns down the hall toward the shop, however, there's a lightness to his step. He'd like to finish the plane. There's house leagues today, but it won't hurt for the team to see how hard it is to win without him.

53

Dear Amy,

I haven't been able to write to you for a while. Every time I've tried, something inside me hurts too much. I know what it is, but it's not fair, Amy. It's not fair. So I push it away again and pretend it's as easy as this, as easy as writing a letter to my best friend.

Yesterday was my birthday. March 4th. We didn't celebrate it last year. This year Mom made a cake and had presents wrapped and sitting on the piano. She's been driving into Winosa whenever the roads are in decent shape.

"Would you like to ask someone over for your birthday supper, Kate?" she asked.

I said no. I could tell she didn't really want me to invite anyone. Part of her didn't want me to have a birthday at all.

Are all of the holidays going to be like this forever, Amy? Is every Christmas or birthday or Easter or Mother's Day or Father's Day going to be something to dread instead of something to look forward to? I never understood that before. I thought when something horrible happened, once it was over that was the worst part. I never knew there were other bad parts that seem to just keep going on and on.

I don't know. I'm tired of trying to make sense of something there is no sense to.

I'm tired of pretending I'm not afraid something else bad will happen. To Mom and Dad. To Aunt Stella. To me.

I'm tired of pretending I'm not mad at Josh. Mad at Josh! How can I be mad at Josh, he didn't want to die! But you know all the times I've talked about being angry at everyone, even though it doesn't make sense? Well, Josh is one of the people I've been angry at too. Because if he was here, things wouldn't be like this. Because if he'd just found some way, some way…

Oh, Amy. If there was a way, he would have found it. I know that!

But sometimes I'm still angry at him.

After we'd blown out the candles on the cake, Mom started to cry.

"I'm sorry," she said. "I thought the second year would be better. Its not. It's like I finally know now he really isn't coming back."

I know what she means Amy. I know. But I want to have holidays again sometime. Not now. But sometime. I'm sorry. I'm sorry.

Remember what I said about there not being such a thing as worse when something is already so bad you can hardly stand it. It's true, but it's not as simple as that. It's different for Mom. I guess it's different for Dad too, wherever he is.

I can't think about it any more. There has to be something else to think about.

Do you remember the time you told me you wanted to be a songwriter when you grew up? We were sitting in your bedroom and it was afternoon and the window was open and the light was lying on the bureau the way it does on summer afternoons. Before you told me you made me promise to never tell. Never, ever tell, because it was too important. If I told, if either of us blabbed about it, it might not happen.

And then you sang me one of the songs you'd written. You wanted me to write it down, not the words—the melody, the music. I'd taken two years of piano and you figured that should be enough for me to be able to write it down.

I never told.

I never wrote it down either.

Maybe I could have if we'd had a piano to figure it out on. Maybe I could have. But I wasn't able to do it just from your singing. I always figured one day at our house we'd sit at the piano and figure it out, but we never did. And now I've forgotten the words. And the tune.

Except just one small part at the beginning…

"In the morning very early when I lie upon my bed,

… voices in my head."

I wish I could remember more.

You're the only songwriter I'll ever know.

54

When he gets home from school, his mom isn't there. Her friend is with Cleo in the apartment.

He has the oddest feeling of detachment. He's at one end of a telescope, his family at the other, the tube sliding longer and longer between them, the distance widening, the focus blurring. Another one gone—his dad, his brother, his mom.

It takes a few minutes before he even hears what the friend is telling him, and then it's only words he catches. Grandmother. Sick. His mother is on an airplane flying across the country to be with her. Not expected to recover.

"She said to tell you she'll be back as soon as she can."

He lets Cleo sit beside him as they watch TV.

The boyfriend comes over and he and his mom's friend talk in the kitchen as they cook dinner.

"It's about the last thing she needs."

"Maybe not. She felt strong enough to fly out. It's good for her to be there."

"But so close to the one year anniversary. Just a few weeks ago."

The word anniversary puzzles Sam for a moment. His mom doesn't celebrate wedding anniversaries. And then suddenly he understands and a feeling of sickness sweeps over him. He didn't know that birthdays and weddings aren't the only anniversary dates people remember year after year. Does this mean it all starts again?

And how guilty do you have to feel if you've let yourself forget.

55

Dear Amy,

I've begun to think of little things about Josh. I want to write them down before I forget.

Omelettes, he made great big omelettes with lots of ketchup on the side and black pepper shaken dark like a storm cloud on top. I can smell the pepper.

Hockey camp, we picked him up after he'd been away for two weeks at hockey camp and he looked different, someone I hadn't seen for a long time, and it was so good to see him and we must have looked that way to him too, because he was full of stories that made us laugh all the way home.

Pimples, I'd just started to get them and he used to tease me. It made me feel rotten, really rotten. I started intercepting messages when his friends called. "Yes, I'll tell him," I'd say, but I'd tell Josh that no one had phoned at all. Josh was sure mad when he found out what I was doing.

You only got mad at me once. It was the day I started teasing Wanda just because everyone always teased Wanda.

"Leave her alone," you told me. "Wanda's OK."

I saw you stand up for her more than once after that. That's how brave you were. You always won too. That's how smart you were.

Every morning when I get out of bed, I look down at my bare feet. My second toe is larger than my big toe. Josh's feet were like that too.

56

His mother returns one evening, walks in the door with her suitcase, gives them each a hug. She looks tired and drained. Her friend wants to stay but his mom sends her home. She takes a few more days off work. Phone calls. Paper work. She talks to Sam sometimes.

"I'm pretty sure she knew me. She was glad I was there," she tells him.

And another time.

"I told her about you and Cleo, about school, about how much you've grown," she says. "She might have understood."

He tries to listen. Who else can she talk to?

"There's a little money," she says. "I didn't think there would be but there is. Enough to pay off what we owe."

He hadn't known they owed money.

In between she just sits. It reminds Sam of the one time Everett was in the hospital, the time his mother made them take him. When she came home from visiting him, she would sit and sit and sit. He and Cleo are extra quiet so as not to disturb her. Is this how the rest of his life is going to be?

On the third day he forgets himself, comes in from school still full of energy from hurrying down the hill, tosses his back pack across the room, knocks over the lamp. It hits the floor with a thump and a crackle of shattered bulb.

His mom appears at the kitchen door. He looks up at her in alarm, the old fear of setting someone off. She shakes her head.

"It's alright, Sam," she says gently. "We've all been through worse than this."

It's like a door has opened and he's found something that's been lost for a long, long time. It's only for a moment, then she's gone back to the kitchen. But if the door opened once, perhaps, it will open again.

He cleans up the mess, replaces the broken bulb.

After supper he lets Cleo talk him into playing Guess. He knows it's okay now if she slaps the cards down hard and laughs when he gives a funny answer.

57

Dear Amy,

I didn't tell you that Jade was having a party. I wasn't going to go except Twyla phoned my mom about it and Mom wanted me to go. She said it would kind of make up for the birthday party that didn't go so well.

Twyla's Dad drove us. We didn't have any trouble finding Jade's house, even though it's a long way east of us, halfway to Winosa. It's built on a hill with a view in three directions. And it's huge.

It's like something you see on TV, Amy, or in magazines like House and Garden. It's two storeys with brick all over and a huge garage and the driveway's all done in stone. The entrance is about as big as my bedroom and the view from the living room looks across the fields for miles. It was just dusk when we got there and the sun setting over the hills was enough to make even Twyla stand there and ohhh and ahhh.

Jade's mom is small and blond with a smile that sparkles. Her Dad is a great, big man with a mustache. He's like a big kid and you can't help but like him right away.

We didn't stay upstairs for long. We went down to the basement where the other kids were, kids from school and kids from Jade's pony club. It's not really a basement with cement and cold walls and that sort of thing. The way their house is built into the hill, three walls are underground but the forth faces outward over the valley with huge glass doors. There's a big-screen TV, and a pool table, and a shuffleboard, and a sound system you can play pretty much as loud as you like because of the way the house is built. There's a gas fireplace that makes everything warm, and pillows and sofas and lots of nooks and corners and a back room where Twyla and Gord disappeared for a long time. Like I said, Twyla better read her own sex book, "P" for prevention. Gord might not be as experienced as Aaron but I've got a feeling that he's trying to catch up, fast.

Ryland and I hung out around the fireplace with everyone else and only disappeared into a nook once. Or maybe twice. But all we did was kiss, which takes a little getting used to but I guess I'm a fast enough learner.

All the boys are nuts about Jade, but she just kind of had a good time with everyone.

It was a fun party. Jade's little brother kept trying to come down and snoop on us, and then her dad would come down and crack a few jokes and carry him away upside down. Sometimes her dad and mom brought food down and talked to us like we were actually real people instead of just a bunch of kids.

Ryland and Travis and some of the others had already gone home when Jade's dad came bounding down the steps two at a time.

"Kill the lights!" he said. "Outside! You can almost hear them crackle!"

It was the Northern Lights, Amy. The great huge, black sky and stars everywhere, a million points of light across an eternity of blackness so that you felt large and small all at the same time, and over top of it all streaks of light growing brighter and brighter until even the stars began to fade.

And they moved, Amy. They'd grow stronger and stronger in one patch, green and white and sometimes almost purple, and they faded in and out across the sky until suddenly, with a wild kind of energy, they streaked tall, tall up to the top of the dome overhead, streaking and swirling and vanishing into blackness again.

What I want to know is this. How can there be something as wonderfully grand as the Northern Lights when there's also such sadness in the world? Is it all part of the same? Does it mean anything? Or is it a trick someone plays, someone without any heart at all?

"I like your dad a lot," I told Jade when we were leaving.

Twyla was saying goodbye to Gord behind the door and Jade and I were standing on the front steps so Twyla's dad would know we'd be there right away.

"He's not my real dad," she said.

"He's not?" I asked.

"He's my stepfather. We moved here to live with him," she said. "Everybody likes him and says I'm really lucky to live in this big house. And it's great. He's great. But I miss my own dad."

I guess now I understand what she said a long time ago, about not being allowed to cry. And I know how she feels about missing her dad.

58

He's been thinking more about Everett, about the way he changed. But he needs help remembering. He thinks he knows a way.

One evening, after he's sure Cleo is asleep, he pulls down the photo albums. It's not the one with Cleo's pictures in it that he opens. It's the other one, the one that comes before that, before Cleo was born.

The first pages are disjointed, the sheets pockmarked by yellow outlines around empty spaces where photographs have been removed. Sometimes half a picture has been reinserted, sometimes a smaller photo from a later date. Sometimes only the empty space remains.

He knows what's happened. There were wedding photographs there once but his mother has pulled the pictures out, the pictures of Everett's father. They never talked of Everett's father.

But she's kept every one of Everett himself, even if she had to cut around his outline with scissors, severing someone's hand here or there. His first steps, his first bicycle. And then, when Everett is maybe six or seven, Sam's dad. Always grinning into the camera. Usually, he notices now, with a can of beer in his hand. Sam's dad hasn't been erased. Maybe she still likes him. Maybe she never had the time to edit him out once things began to unravel.

And pretty soon baby pictures of Sam himself. Everett helping Sam to walk. Everett playing soccer with him. He's right. It's a house. It's small but there's a yard and trees.

Two brothers. Sam never thought of Everett as a half brother. Two brothers. My big brother Everett.

It's hard to know for sure, of course, but everything in the pictures says that for these split seconds—the time it takes a camera shutter to click, maybe even for a few seconds longer, maybe for a few days or months or even a few years—things were OK. Maybe they were even good.

But not for much longer. Not for much longer. Sam closes the book when he finds a picture of Everett pushing him on a swing.

The images are still rushing through his brain like a slide show when he goes to bed and he needs to find some way to turn them off in order to get to sleep. Frozen soul.

59

Dear Amy,

I'm still not sure what really happened.

We had a tremendous snowstorm and the buses were sent home early from school, not because it was cold, but because of the heavy kind of snow that was falling. It took us hours and hours to get home. Our bus got stuck three times. The older boys helped Mrs. Gilbert chain up and dig out. The closer we got to home, the fewer the farms and the fewer people there were on the bus to help.

Finally, on the last long stretch from Twyla's farm to our place, a drift at the corner caught the bus yet again. I walked up to the front seat.

"Can I help you out?" I asked Mrs. Gilbert as she began to haul out the chains.

"You sure could, Kate. You could do me a real big favour," she said. "Roddy needs help practicing his reading. There's never enough time, and tonight's going to be another lost cause. Could you just listen while he reads to you?"

"Sure," I said. "But won't you need help outside?"

"I think help is on the way," she said.

I looked up the road thinking a snowplough or some-one with a four-wheel drive was coming, but the only thing on the road was the blowing snow and the settling dusk. Mrs. Gilbert clambered down the steps. Just as she let herself through the door I saw someone on horseback approaching out of the woods at the side of the bus. The figure in the saddle was bulky and obscure beneath a mound of winter clothing, and the horse was big and muscular, as tall as Mr. Limster's Sampson and maybe even taller, stepping strongly through the snow.

Mrs. Gilbert pushed the door shut to keep the heat in and then all I could see were shadows beyond the frosted windows of the bus. Her little boy slid across the seat and looked up at me, half shy, half hopeful.

Roddy is as sweet as his cookie-crumb freckles. I thought he'd complain about having to read, but he didn't. I guess he hasn't been worn down by years of school yet. He still thinks reading is some kind of magic trick, like pulling rabbits out of hats.

It was dark and snowing harder than ever when I started up the lane. The house was dark too, and as I let myself in the phone was ringing.

"Kate? Kate?"

"It's me, Mom. Where are you?"

"I'm in Winosa. The roads are closed. I don't know if I can even make it home tonight."

"It's OK Mom," I told her. "I'm OK. I'll take care of myself."

"Don't go out to the barn. Stay in the house. The horses will be OK just for a night and I don't want…"

The weight of the snow must have brought the lines down because the phone went dead.

I didn't go out to the barn. I didn't have to. Just as I was getting dressed I looked out the window and saw the same horse and rider pushing through the snow up the driveway. Now that I had a better look at them it seemed to me that it wasn't just a horse as big as Sampson, it was Sampson.

And if the horse was Sampson, the rider had to be Dad. Didn't it have to be Dad? Except whoever it was had so many layers of clothing I couldn't tell for sure.

He saw me at the window and motioned to me to stay, then turned Sampson towards the barn and a few minutes later the lights came on.

I wanted to go to the barn, but I was scared. Not scared of who was out there, just scared it wasn't really Dad, that it was a dream, that I was imagining it. Scared that if I went out there he'd go away forever and never return. I know it's crazy Amy, but that's how I felt. I couldn't leave the house. It was like some kind of magic spell.

There was no truck in the yard. No sign of him around the house. The lights were on in the barn all night, or at least as long as I was awake. I sat in a chair by the window and dozed and watched and dozed. Every time I woke there was the darkness and the snow and the light in the barn.

The last doze was a long one. It was daylight when I woke. The storm had stopped. The spell was broken. I dressed and hurried out to the barn. The horses looked at me with disinterest. They'd been fed and watered and everything put in its place.

Behind the barn I could see two freshly broken trails through the snow. One was where a horse had been let back into the pasture. The other was a person's track. I stepped into it. The holes in the snow were big and deep and wide apart so that I had to stretch to place my boot within, exactly as I'd had to do the night of the memorial service, the night I'd thought Mr. Hanks had done the chores alone.

At the corner where the wooden corral is replaced by barbed wire fencing, the wind swept the tracks away. By the time Mom got home that afternoon all signs of horse and rider were gone and life went on exactly as it had been.

Maybe I imagined it all.

60

They both hear the thunk on the window but it's Cleo who goes over to look.

"It's a bird," she says. "It's just lying there, Sam."

He's in the middle of a TV show he actually likes to watch. And he's seen birds hit the window before.

"It's only had the wind knocked out if it," he tells her. "In a few minutes it'll get up and fly away."

Cleo doesn't leave the window.

"It's not going to get up Sam," she says.

He goes to look. The bird is no longer there, the real bird, that is. Only the shell remains, feathers and beak and legs. Cleo stares and stares but when she looks at Sam her eyes are completely dry.

"Your hamster," she says. "It wasn't sleeping, was it Sam?"

Everett. A few years ago. So much for Cleo not understanding.

It's another place Sam doesn't want to go, but he remembers anyway, sees the cuff of a green sweater, hears the clank of a garbage bin. He had to get rid of it quickly, afraid it would set Everett off in some other direction. It's only a hamster, Sam.

"I know what we'll do," he says. "That little box the tea was in. Mom finished it this morning."

They're in the middle of a city in an apartment without a backyard, but Sam knows a place. He has the odd little feeling that he's used the spot before, even though he knows he's never buried a bird. Didn't have time to bury the hamster. The box is small and they place it inside a bag as well, so no one will ask what they are doing.

Together they walk to the park. There was a big snow-storm a few days ago, but already most of it is gone. It's easy to get to the little bush that stands at the far corner. It's the loose rocks along the base he remembers. No need for a shovel.

It doesn't take long. They remove some rocks and almost by magic make a little cave beneath where they can place the box and return the rocks without crushing it. It's sad, but it's a good place for the shell of a small bird, outside with the trees and the grass.

On the way back Cleo takes his hand.

"Thank you, Sam," she says.

He nods and he's grateful.

But all of a sudden something else is happening too. He knows why he thought he'd used the spot before. It was the hiding place he almost used for the gun.

The park. It was the first place he thought of as he went racing down the stairs and out of the apartment with his heart pounding in his ears. Ditch the gun in the park. Why not the river? Why didn't he just run to the river and toss it in? Or the pond? He doesn't know. Maybe they both just seemed too far. Maybe he wasn't thinking straight.

He got to the park and then he had to find somewhere to hide it. The rocks. He'd hide it in the rocks down at the far end where they'd put the new bushes in. But as soon as he got there and bent to shift the rocks, he knew he was being watched.

Chalmers! Chalmers had been watching him from the

edge of the trees. How could his mind trick him this way? How could it have forgotten that Chalmers had followed him?

All he'd wanted then was to get out of sight. Get somewhere that he couldn't be seen. Back over the grass, across the other street, down the back alley, duck in the overgrown yard at the corner where the house was already boarded up and waiting. Just because he'd been out of sight doesn't mean he hadn't been followed there as well.

Chalmers hasn't been bluffing. He knows where Sam took the gun.

Now what is he going to do?

61

Dear Amy,

Someone is staying in the cabin across the valley. I'm not sure how long they've been there but it could be since the day of the memorial service in February, it could easily be since then and I just never noticed things before. On calm days I see smoke rising above the trees and when it's very quiet I can hear the bite of an axe chopping wood. I've tried using the binoculars to see who it is but the driveway and the front door to the cabin are on the side away from our farm. Mr. Hanks must know who it is.

"Ellie, I promise I won't be mad," I say at least once a day at school. "Tell me who's staying at the Turlow place."

"I told you," says Ellie. "It's just some friend of theirs. Who else would it be?"

And maybe that's who it really is. Or maybe that's all she knows.

But I know who I want it to be. When I come home from school, especially when Mom's been to Winosa for the afternoon the way she's doing it again, now that the weather is better, I watch for signs that he's been here. I look for an extra set of wheel tracks in our yard, a bucket out of place in the barn or some sign that Sherbrooke has had company. Sometimes I'm sure he's been here. Other times I think I'm imagining things.

It would be easy to find out the truth. The snow's settled now and the winter horses have been all over that part of the field, packing it down. I could walk to the cabin. But I don't. Mom would wonder why I'm traipsing off through the field. I don't want her to wonder. I don't want her to ask. What if I'm wrong?

And if it is him, then what am I supposed to do? Should I be madder than ever at him? For being here without telling us? For staying just that far away without even letting us know? How could he do that? I've every right to be madder than ever.

But you know what, Amy? I don't want to be mad any more. Being mad only helps the hurting for a while. After that it's no good any more, something else has to happen. I don't know what, but something. It's not simple. It's never simple.

I haven't told Mom anything.

Its like we're all frozen in time, frozen into a winter that seems to never end. But at school things keep happening. Ryland bought me a bracelet—thin and silver and beautiful.

"I can't take it," I told him.

He was pretty upset.

"I thought we liked each other," he said.

"We do," I said. "I just don't think it's a good idea for me to take it, that's all."

"It's just a present," he said. "It doesn't mean you owe me anything."

"Doesn't it?" I asked.

"It doesn't have to," he said.

"Good," I said. "But I'm still not taking it. Let's just say I don't want to jinx things."

"Jinx things how?" asked Ryland. "Did you have an old boyfriend who gave you something and then dumped you?"

An old boyfriend who dumped me. The worst he thinks could have happened in my life. I almost laughed. I almost cried. You know, Amy, Ryland doesn't really know me. None of them know me here. I've been trying so hard to keep my head above water, that's the only me they know. Maybe I'm more like Mom than I like to admit, when I'm not falling apart I'm carrying on as if everything is fine and dandy, as if I always change schools, always make friends, always have boyfriends.

It's like I've made myself into someone else, someone who rides horses and takes care of her mom and stands up for Norm Smith (I really did do that the other day. The grade nine girls were picking on him and I just walked up and said quietly "Come on Norm, let's go where the air's better." You would have been proud of me.) I'm playing on the basketball team. (In a school as small as this one, all the tall kids get to play, but I'm better than I thought I would be!) I'm helping Roddy learn to read and I've managed to be friends with Carolyn and Jade and Ellie and Twyla all at the same time, which isn't easy except I seem to know something that other kids don't. I seem to know what isn't important, and what is.

But it isn't me, Amy. It isn't all of me. A huge part is missing. I know I can't ever have that part back again, but I'm not sure how much longer I can keep pretending it never happened at all. Or even that half of it happened and half of it didn't.

And there has to be a way for Dad to come back to the farm. Mom was right. I've seen him work the horses. This is where Dad should be.

62

When he goes out on Sunday, he sees Chalmers dart from the alley behind the abandoned house and make a beeline straight for him.

"Sammy boy! We got better things to do. Let's do a little explore."

Sam keeps walking. Chalmers laughs, falls in beside him.

"You're coming around to see things my way, aren't you. That's good. We can be friends again. Buddies at school. I've seen you in the halls. You can use a buddy or two!"

"It's not there," he says. "I moved it. Long time ago."

Chalmers shakes his head.

"You're a lousy liar," he says. "I can tell. I know stuff, Sammy. I know what you're like. You kid yourself, Sammy. You think you're different. You're not. But you need someone to help you along."

Sam keeps walking, glad of how strong his legs have become. Chalmers has to do a half jog to keep up.

"Look, this is no big deal. What harm can it do? I'll take care of it. It's me. You've known me forever. I'm not like your brother. All that yelling and screaming. I'm not like that. You ever seen me like that? And you sure don't want to pick it up yourself. The way you raced out into the hall with it wrapped up in a ball cap for crying out loud. As if that would hide anything."

Sam just keeps walking. Chalmers is puffing now.

"Look, you don't have to go near the place. Just help me

out by telling me where it is. I'll take care of it. Just between you and me, Sam."

Chalmers is having a hard, hard time keeping up.

"It's worth a lot, Sam. Those guys that hang out on the corner by the store. It's worth a lot in more ways than one. And I'm going to find it anyway. I'm not going to stop looking."

Sam's legs are a long way from being tired and he's pulling swiftly out of range. But the voice follows Sam, a small dirty wind between the rush of traffic.

"If you're saving it to use yourself, forget it. I'll be watching. I'll know."

Sam realizes he can't wait much longer. But he still can't decide what happens next.

63

Dear Amy,

I've remembered another couple of lines to the song you wrote.

"In the morning, very early, when I lie within my bed. Sounds of city, sounds of people, voices calling in my head. And I want to sleep forever, but I get right up instead. Life's too precious, life's too lovely, to be wasted."

Oh, Amy.

64

For two nights he doesn't sleep. The third night, although the plan seems incredible to him at first, he knows what he's going to do.

All day he waits and waits and waits. When school is over he intercepts him right after class, hustles him out the back door of the school, gets him halfway down the alley before anyone can see. John Keily.

"I need you to do something," he tells John. "Don't ask. Just listen. It's important. I can't do it. If I make a mistake and they figure out it's me it's not going to be simple. Our family has had too much trouble. I need you to tell the police. I need you to tell them where it is."

He's printed the address of the abandoned house on a piece of paper. Underneath he's made a map of the location, behind a broken slat between the walls in the front entrance. That's why Chalmers hasn't found it. He's been looking in the house but Sam never got inside. He didn't have any idea how to break in. He'd just needed to get out of sight. He'd hidden himself in the front entrance, just sat there for a long, long time, until maybe his heart wasn't beating quite so fast. And then he'd found the broken slat in the wall with a space just big enough.

"It's a gun," he says.

The look on John's face tells him all.

"It's not THE gun," he says quickly. "It's from before that, from when my brother was still at home. The time Mom made them take him to the hospital. Someone knows it's there, they just don't know where exactly. But they'll look until they find it. They mustn't find it. "

John is staring at him, staring and staring.

"It's the best I can think of, to let the cops get rid of it," says Sam. "Too much has happened already. No more. Enough. Whatever began has to stop happening."

Still John does not answer.

"After you tell them where it is, you can do anything to me that you want," says Sam. "You can beat me up if you want to. You can say it all right to my face. I'm glad your brother's dead. Why didn't he kill himself first instead of afterward? How come you didn't know it was going to happen? Why couldn't your family stop him? Are you all nuts? Are you going to kill people too? I hate your whole family. You're a bunch of monsters."

He's run out of things to say. All he can do is stand there.

After a lifetime, John puts the paper in his pocket.

"It would be easier if you were some kind of monster," he says. "That's one of the hard parts. There's nobody to hate."

He turns and walks away.

It's only when he's gone that Sam realizes he has no way at all of knowing what he'll really do with the information.

65

Dear Amy,

I didn't know it would come so quickly, spring, I mean. Just last week it was still winter but now the snow seems to have vanished overnight and there's water running everywhere. The horses search the pastures for green grass and Sherbrooke searches for gophers.

Mom and I have begun to pack. It's what has to be done. We can take care of the horses, but we can't train them for Mr. Limster. And Mom has found people in Winosa, people who understand some of what she's going through because they've been through it themselves, one way or another.

"It's not the same," I told her. "How could it be the same as what happened at the Quick Mart?"

"They're all sad stories," said Mom. "They aren't the same, but we can feel for each other."

Which I guess is another way of saying there isn't "worse" when the hurting is so bad you can't stand it. There's different, but there isn't worse. Mom says they talk about things and it helps, the talking and the having someone really listening, helps.

She's found a job, too, so next week we're moving, not all the way back to the city, just to Winosa. That's OK by me. I needed so badly to stay here after Christmas. Now, just as badly it seems, I need to leave.

"So long as we don't have to keep Josh's death a secret any more," I said.

"No more secrets," said Mom.

It's not true, but it will have to do for now.

Yesterday, when I knew Ellie had gone to visit her cousins, I rode over and told Mr. Hanks we're moving.

"I don't like it," said Mr. Hanks. "Families need to stay together, especially when there's trouble."

Which made me think again that Mr. Hanks must have offered the Turlow place to Dad, but even then I couldn't just ask him if Dad was there. I had to kind of walk around it, as if it wasn't even important.

"I thought you might know someone who could come take care of the horses, someone who knows what to do," I said. "If you do, they should phone Mr. Limster right away."

"I hear you," said Mr. Hanks. "But I wish there was another way. Sometimes it just takes time."

And sometimes it just takes doing the best you can. That's what I think. And this is doing the best I can.

In a week, maybe a little bit more, we'll be gone. I'm scared again, Amy. It'll be better for Mom and it'll be better for Dad, but what about me? I can't keep writing letters forever. It isn't fair. It isn't fair to either of us.

But it hurts so much, Amy. So much.

66

It's Saturday when the phone rings. Cleo answers it.

"Ellen?" she asks into the receiver. "I don't think my brother knows anyone named Ellen. Are you sure you want to talk to him?"

Sam motions to Cleo to hand over the phone. She shrugs and passes across to him. He goes into his bedroom and closes the door.

"Hélène?" he asks.

"I don't usually do this kind of thing," she says. "Pass messages between people."

He waits for her to continue.

"But maybe this is a different kind of circumstance," she says. "That thing you wanted John to tell the cops about, he said to let you know that they found it. He called back and made sure. They didn't hassle him. And it was exactly where you told him it would be."

"Good," says Sam. "That's good."

Hélène is still on the line. Waiting.

"He told you what it was, didn't he," says Sam.

"Does it matter?" asks Hélène.

"He told you," says Sam. "He wasn't supposed to tell."

"Like I said, I don't do the go-between thing unless there's a good reason." He can tell something's bothering her. He can hear the tiniest bit of a French accent. He's never heard that before.

And she's still waiting.

"What?" asks Sam.

"You can't just not talk about something like this," she says. "I don't care how long ago it was or how up tight and English someone is, you can't just not talk about things."

He doesn't know what to say. He doesn't hang up either.

"Was it loaded?"

"No," says Sam. "Not when I hid it. I mean, it was at first. It all happened so fast. I was just looking for something he'd taken from me. And I found it. And Mom saw me with it and right away she took the bullets out. And Everett caught her. And after that I don't know, I don't know. I just grabbed it and left."

For a long time the only sound on the phone is silence. This time it's Sam's own voice that sounds odd in his ears.

"It wasn't good living with him, Hélène. I loved him because he was my brother, but it wasn't good. I can't ever end up like him. I can't."

Another long silence.

"Whatever he was like, you're not the same as your brother, Sam," says Hélène at last. "You're a different person."

And then, gently, she hangs up.

67

Dear Amy,

Some people say the bad things in life are put there to make you appreciate the good things. I don't think that's true. I think the people who say that just never had anything really bad happen to them.

But good things do happen sometimes.

Early this morning, Sand Dancer had her colt.

I thought I was the only one who guessed it might be time, and even then it took me a while to realize what I'd seen. Yesterday morning there were waxy-looking drops on Sand Dancer's bag, where the colt will suck. I saw them out of the corner of my eye while I was cleaning her stall, but I didn't understand at first. She isn't supposed to foal for weeks yet. But I saw the drops and all day they were kind of at the back of my mind. Hadn't I read something about drops like that in one of Dad's horse books over Christmas, when I'd been trying not to think of anything at all? But now I was thinking about everything else too, about moving, about saying goodbye to the kids at school, about how Ellie had promised to watch out for Nelson and Sherbrooke after we're gone.

And then at three o'clock in the morning I remembered. I'm not kidding. It was three o'clock in the morning and pitch dark and I sat upright in my bed and remembered. Those waxy drops form just before a mare foals. I slipped into my clothes and headed out to the barn to check on her.

"Hello, Kate."

The voice came out of the blackness beside the barn door. I jumped a foot but I didn't yell or anything, although it felt like I yelled because my heart was beating so strongly in my ears.

"Dad?" I asked.

He took a step forward. The yard light spilled across him. He looked thinner than I remembered, like a dish rag that's been through the wash a million times.

"It's me," he said. "I'm sorry. I seem to have got in the habit of skulking around."

I didn't say anything. I couldn't think of what to say. Dad put a hand on my shoulder.

"I know," he said. "I've let you down. I'm sorry."

But it's like I said, Amy. I don't want to be angry any more.

"You didn't let anyone down," I said. "You came back. You just couldn't tell us."

He gave my shoulder a squeeze. That's about as close as Dad gets to a hug.

"Is Sand Dancer OK?" I asked. "She's ready to foal isn't she?"

"I think so," said Dad. "She seemed restless so I left her for a bit. A lot of mares just like to handle things on their own. But we can take a look now if you like."

We went quietly into the barn. Dad had left a light on at the back. Sand Dancer had been lying down, the way a mare does when it foals, but as we approached she stood up and began to walk again. Walk and paw, walk and paw and swing her head towards her back end. I could feel my insides begin to churn, because even I could tell something was wrong.

"Kate," said Dad softly. "Do you think you can sneak

into the house without your Mom hearing and get a bucket of warm water, a bar of soap, and clean towels?"

"No," I said.

Dad looked at me. I took a slow, deep breath.

"It wouldn't be fair. She's been helping with the horses too," I said. "But I could go in and wake her up and tell her what I'm doing."

Dad seemed to weigh my words for a moment. If he was thinking I'd changed lately, he was right. I wouldn't have said that to him three months ago.

"Alright," he said. Sand Dancer pawed the hay restlessly. "Be quick."

And I was quick. And so was Mom. She was sound asleep and I'm sure she thought I was crazy when I told her Sand Dancer was having trouble foaling and Dad was in the barn to help, but for once Mom's ability to set aside her feelings and spring into action was exactly right. She and I were back in the barn in double time.

"I think it's just a hoof turned backward."

That's what Dad said after he'd felt around a little. It's pretty gross to describe and it's pretty weird to watch, especially when you're holding the tail the way I was, but after Dad washed up he reached right inside the mare to try to find out what was going wrong.

And it was a hoof, Amy—one little hoof that was turned backward. Colts are born front hooves first and if one of them is turned backward the mare has an awful time. Dad was able to help her. He was able to shift the colt right inside the mare just enough so that he could carefully pull the hoof the right way round.

It was gross to watch but it was wonderful too, because after that it happened so fast. There was part of a colt and then all of the colt, a real live colt all wet and gooey, and when it actually gave a kick my heart just about flew out of me because we knew then it was alive. Alive! And I was laughing and crying all at the same time.

Dad and I helped Sand Dancer after that. She was pretty tired. I carefully pulled the colt over closer to her head and cleared some of the membranes with the towels. Dad smeared some of the colt smell onto Sand Dancer's nose. Pretty soon Sand Dancer was licking it all over and you could see it was like a tonic for them both. Dad and I stood back with Mom and just watched and watched.

"It's quite a sight, isn't it?" said Dad.

"It's beautiful," said Mom. "Josh would have loved to see it."

Oh no, I thought. Please no. Not now. No. Not over and over and over. And I waited for Dad to turn away.

But I guess he's changed a bit over the last couple of months as well. Dad may look worn out, but he's stronger, too, in a way I can't explain.

"Maybe he can see it," said Dad. "Not the way we do, but maybe some way."

And then I surprised myself. I said, "Maybe Amy can see it too."

Did you see it, Amy? Were you in the barn when the colt was born? I don't know what happens after death. No one knows. But it doesn't matter. You don't really have to have been there. It's just another way of thinking about things.

A gentler way. It doesn't have to be right. It's just a way of thinking, a way of being able to carry the pain.

And I've wanted to say it so badly. Your name. Out loud.

It was the first time I've been able to say your name out loud since you died with Josh at the Quick Mart.

68

He thought he'd have to put up with Chalmers hounding him for months and months afterward, maybe forever because what proof could there be that the gun was gone?

But he only had to say it once. One time—at school the next week when Chalmers was waiting for him by the back door and cornered him.

"I told the cops," Sam said. "It's gone."

Once. He didn't even have to repeat it. Chalmers knew that this time Sam was telling the truth.

Chalmers swore and told Sam he was an idiot. And then he forgot about him. Sam, the non-person. Not forever, Sam's sure. Somewhere down the line Chalmers will think of some other way Sam might be of use to him. They're still at the same school. They still live only a few blocks apart.

"Now can we go, Sam. Please?"

Cleo has been pestering him all afternoon to take her to the park. He decides to give in. It's a good day to be outside. Everywhere is spring and greenery. He's only begun to know some of the layers that have built up inside him over the years, only had a glimpse of the things that are hiding there. But one tiny part of him is quiet and still.

Hélène is right. He's a different person from his brother. When he came up with a plan for the gun, it was something Everett never would have done. He's going to try to trust himself in other ways as well.

"Give me an under-duck Sam!" cries Cleo.

He lifts the swing just the smallest bit higher, ducks gently beneath it, and sends her sailing safely, swiftly up into the air.

69

Dear Amy,

It's July, and a long time since I've written. For a little while, just saying your name was all I could manage. Then I told Nelson and Sherbrooke about you. And then I told Ellie.

I told her about Josh, how much I loved him, and love him still, even if we weren't the perfect brother and sister every moment of the time.

And I told her about you, and that you were my best friend.

She didn't know what to say, but she listened. She was a good place to begin.

I'm still here on the farm. It's taken time to sort things out. It's taken time for everyone to figure out how to begin to fit the pieces together the best we can.

Mom's living in Winosa on her own. She phones every night. She drives out every weekend. On the days she comes out, sometimes things go pretty good between her and Dad. Sometimes you can tell it's harder.

It's that way for me too.

I don't know if we'll ever, all three of us, live together full time again. But I know we'll never be apart either.

Since that day in the barn, Dad hasn't said a single word about Josh. Mom says she's learned that some people are like that when a person they love dies. They can't talk about it, but it doesn't mean they don't care. They find other ways to be sad, other ways to remember. I think she's right. I see Dad leaning against the truck on days when he hasn't got any intention of driving anywhere at all, and I know he's thinking about Josh.

And at least he talks to me again, talks to me like I'm really here and listening, which I am. Yesterday I was leaning on the fence laughing at something funny Sand Dancer's colt was doing and he came and stood beside me.

"I'm sure glad we've still got you, Kate," he said.

Did you whisper in his ear to say that, Amy? Did you know it was exactly what I needed to hear?

Mom told me something else. It was hard for her, but you have to do all the hard parts too. That's what it seems like anyway. You can't just do some of the hard parts and walk away. I tried, but I couldn't. Mom tried, but she couldn't. You have to do all of the hard parts.

She told me you came to the house that morning.

"Amy came to the house and you were still in the shower, Kate." That's what Mom said. "I invited her to come inside and wait for you but…"

I had to wait for the next bit. Mom took a long gulp of air. It felt like we were both drowning.

"I wasn't as welcoming as I might have been, Kate. I invited her in, but I didn't smile and joke and pull her through the door the way I would have done with any of your other friends."

Oh Amy, I knew that's what happened. I didn't want to know, but I knew. You were supposed to come over that morning. I didn't know what time, but I knew you were coming. And it's the way Mom always was with you. Polite—but never more than polite.

You didn't come in. You headed down to the corner store to talk to Josh. You liked Josh. Everyone liked Josh. If only you hadn't liked him!

But that isn't fair either because you would have gone to the store anyway, because it was the day after Valentines Day and you knew they'd be on for half price. We discovered that a long time ago when our allowances wouldn't stretch far enough. We could get them half price the day after Valentines's Day. We both loved them. Cinnamon hearts. For us. For two best friends.

"I will wish," said Mom, "I will wish, forever, that I'd made her feel welcome enough to come inside to wait."

And I will wish it too, Amy. Just like I will wish I'd warned Josh about the dream I never had.

It won't do any good, but I will wish it too.

And all along I have been wishing, wishing I was writing the kind of letters that could really be mailed, wishing some day I'd receive a letter back and discover it's all been a mistake and that you're coming to visit, wishing you could meet the kids I've talked about in the letters.

They aren't close friends the way you and I were, but I like them. I've kept in touch with them over the summer. Twyla's visiting her sister in the city. Jade's going to ritzy Pony Club classes that her stepdad is paying for. Carolyn's at leadership training camp, I hope they teach her to lead without being quite so bossy. And Mr. Limster left Nelson here after all, so Ellie and I are riding every day. We've even started to learn how to work our horses in the show ring.

I guess that just leaves Ryland. It's pretty hard to have a boyfriend on a farm when neither of us is old enough to drive, so we've pretty much decided just to be friends. He still wants me to take the silver bracelet, though. He says that gypsies have offered him big money for it and I'd better say yes now or it's gone. We talk on the phone.

I still wish you were here. I wish Josh was here too. And I'm sorry, I'm so sorry for what happened. I don't know any answers. I'd like to try and do something that would help, help make it so that awful things don't happen to other people, other families, other friends. I can't yet, but I would like to sometime.

And sometime, soon, I'm going to write your mom a letter, just so she'll know other people are thinking about you too. She's still in the same house. I phoned Megan and found out that much at least. Your mom didn't run away like we did, Amy. Your mom is strong. She and your grandmother are both strong. Our old school has made a garden in the courtyard for everybody to enjoy and there's a little fountain where your mom and grandma take care of the flowers all around.

And if it helps, there's something I know now. It's important to me. Maybe it's important to you too.

There is a little part of you that will always be with me. It will be with me when I go back to school next year, and the years after, and when I graduate and go on to whatever it is I end up doing. That little part will be writing songs in the back of my mind and turning cartwheels and standing up for people who can't stand up for themselves. It will be helping me to see the world differently. It will be helping me not to waste what comes along.

And sometimes there will still be bad days, awful days

when everything will seem so grey and thick and pointless it will be hard to think and care and move. But there will be better days as well. And some days I will write to you, like now, when there is something I have to share with the friend who always understood me best.

I had another dream last night. We were sitting side by side on the bank under the tree at Third Bend. You looked at me and you smiled. It was your "we can do it" smile.

"Stop worrying about me, Kate," you said. "I'm OK."

Oh Amy, it's still awful. It's still wrong. It will always be wrong. I'm still so sorry. But it made me feel, for the first time, that there really is something called tomorrow.

I'll always think of you.

I'll always think of you.

I'll always think of you.

Your forever friend,

Kate